Sofia Acosta

MAKES A
SCENE

Sofia Acosta
MAKES A SCENE

Emma Otheguy

Alfred A. Knopf
New York

Text copyright © 2022 by Emma Otheguy
Jacket art copyright © 2022 by Mirelle Ortega

All rights reserved. Published in the United States by Alfred A. Knopf, an imprint of Random House Children's Books, a division of Penguin Random House LLC, New York.

Knopf, Borzoi Books, and the colophon are registered trademarks of Penguin Random House LLC.

Visit us on the Web! rhcbooks.com

Educators and librarians, for a variety of teaching tools, visit us at
RHTeachersLibrarians.com

Library of Congress Cataloging-in-Publication Data
Names: Otheguy, Emma, author.
Title: Sofía Acosta makes a scene
Description: First edition. | New York: Alfred A. Knopf, 2022. | Audience: Ages 8–12. | Audience: Grades 4–6. | Summary: Sofía Acosta, a fifth grader trying to fit into her ballet-obsessed Cuban American family and her affluent suburban New York community, learns to speak up for herself and others when she mistakenly reveals a visiting dancer's plan to defect to the United States.
Identifiers: LCCN 2021021658 (print) | LCCN 2021021659 (ebook) |
ISBN 978-0-593-37263-0 (hardcover) | ISBN 978-0-593-37264-7 (library binding) |
ISBN 978-0-593-37265-4 (ebook)
Subjects: CYAC: Ballet dancing—Fiction. | Emigration and immigration—Fiction. | Handicraft—Fiction. | Family life—New York (State)—Fiction. | Social classes—Fiction. | Cuban Americans—Fiction. | LCGFT: Novels.
Classification: LCC PZ7.1.O87 So 2022 (print) | LCC PZ7.1.O87 (ebook) |
DDC [Fic]—dc23

The text of this book is set in 11.5-point Maxime Pro.
Interior design by Cathy Bobak
Jacket design by Sylvia Bi

Printed in the United States of America
January 2022
10 9 8 7 6 5 4 3 2 1

First Edition

Para mi Alaya Luz,
te quiero con el alma

CHAPTER ONE

Tricia and I are holding left pinkies under our desks, which always works. It's how we managed to be the only fifth graders to have been in the same class every single year of elementary school: we held left pinkies under the desks whenever a teacher talked about the next year. Now it's Thursday after school and Mrs. Kalinack, the school secretary, is visiting our classroom to talk about the epic party she's organizing for our teacher, Mr. Fallon. Mr. Fallon is from Ireland but has been teaching at Pine Hill Elementary for years. Over the summer, he became a United States citizen. Mrs. Kalinack says that means he belongs in the country as much as anyone who was born here, and he has new rights and responsibilities. That's the boring part.

The exciting part is that our school is going to throw a big party to congratulate him. There are going to be flag cupcakes and red-white-and-blue decorations, and the gym will hardly look like a school gym by the time we finish. Mrs. Kalinack is assigning the fifth graders to committees, and Tricia and I are trying to get on the Decorations Committee together. That's the best one. (Some people are going to be assigned to the Cleanup Committee. Those are kids who don't believe in left pinkies, even though we told everyone else to try it. We're nice that way.)

Mr. Fallon has no idea what we're planning; the party is going to be a complete surprise. Mrs. Kalinack has come up with all sorts of excuses to keep Mr. Fallon away while we work on the party, and everyone who volunteers is going to have to meet during some lunch periods and stay late after school a few times. This is exciting, because usually after school I have to pick up my little brother, Manuel, from the second/third-grade door and walk him home so we can both do our homework and get ready for ballet class. If Tricia and I are on the Decorations Committee together, we'll get to hang out after school, and maybe my older sister, Regina, will have to pick up Manuel for a change.

"Tricia Rivera—you applied for the Decorations Committee. No problem," Mrs. Kalinack says. Tricia squeals and lets go of my pinky to hug Stella, who is sitting on the other side of us and already got picked for captain of the Decorations Committee. But as soon as she and Stella finish hugging and cheering, along with Abdul and Lucas, who are also on the Decorations Committee, Tricia turns back and links pinkies with me.

Mrs. Kalinack is going through all the names in reverse alphabetical order to be fair to people with *Z* names, so it takes forever to get to me. "Sofía Acosta," she says finally, "you applied for the Decorations Committee."

"Yep," I say confidently.

"Aren't you going to be very busy with *The Nutcracker* the next few weeks?"

Tricia and I look at each other, and she shakes her head. She knows what I'm thinking. There are four other kids in the fifth grade who do ballet, including Tricia. But teachers only worry about how much time it will take *me*, because my parents are performing arts teachers at the high school and my older sister is practically a professional and, well, the Acosta family is a big part of *The Nutcracker* in this town. But I do *The Nutcracker* every year. Mr. Fallon is only going to become a United States citizen once. I definitely want to do the Decorations Committee with Tricia. I tell Mrs. Kalinack that, but she purses her lips.

"We already have several volunteers for Decorations. But the History and Contexts Committee is a little thin. It's just Laura, the captain. No one else has signed up."

That's because Laurita is only interested in two things: softball and protests. If you work with her at school, she'll give you an earful about the polar ice caps melting or make you listen to her talk about batting statistics.

"I won't let ballet get in the way," I promise Mrs. Kalinack. "And I bet I could help make the gym look really nice. . . ."

Tricia drops my pinky, as if she already knows it's over.

Mrs. Kalinack doesn't even respond. "That's decided, then: Sofía's working with Laura. Our meeting times are on the schedules I emailed to your parents. Remember, don't tell Mr. Fallon! You have no idea the time I've had making sure he isn't around during our meetings, so no one give it away."

Around me, chairs scrape against the floor as people get up and grab their backpacks. Everyone is talking and making plans with the other kids in their groups, but I'm just sitting there.

"I guess you should go talk to Laura," Tricia says. "It'll probably be an interesting committee—didn't Mrs. Kalinack say the History and Contexts people were going to put up, like, an exhibit around the gym?"

My eyes sting and I can't think of anything to say. Tricia and I have been talking about the Decorations Committee since we first found out about this party. We were going to make foam cutouts of every state and then decorate them with sequins and rhinestones so the gym would sparkle. I pack up my backpack and wait around for everyone to leave, and then I shuffle up to Mrs. Kalinack.

"You don't want to miss your bus." Mrs. Kalinack tucks her papers into a folder and puts Mr. Fallon's stool back in the corner where he usually keeps it.

"I'm a walker, remember?" I only live two blocks from the school. "I wanted to talk to you about my assignment—you see, I'm pretty good at sewing and crafts and stuff. The Decorations Committee might need my help."

Mrs. Kalinack pulls down her reading glasses. I've known Mrs. Kalinack since kindergarten, and that isn't a good sign. She does not like excuses. Come to school late without a note and that's the end of you. My face gets hot the minute she pulls off those glasses.

"Sofía Acosta, what grade are you in now?"

"Umm, fifth?" This seems obvious.

"Don't you think that by fifth grade, individuals should be mature enough that they don't complain about not getting their first choice of everything? Just imagine Sarah Zimmerman; she never gets to pick first, and do you see her complaining?"

"Well, she got to pick first today, actually—"

I think smoke might come out of Mrs. Kalinack's nose soon. She's breathing like an angry dragon. Between that and the glasses, I know it's time to drop it.

"Sofía, no more complaints from you. Besides, isn't Laura Sánchez your neighbor? It'll be much easier for the two of you to work together, and you'll need to do some things outside of school; that was part of the agreement when you signed up to help plan the party."

Mrs. Kalinack swings her messenger bag over her shoulder and gathers up her folder. She holds open the door for me.

Outside, everyone is lining up for buses or looking for

their friends and heading to the playground. I have to go to the second/third-grade door to get Manuel before he finds like six playdates for Friday, which is the only day we don't have ballet. My mom says everyone is always welcome at our house, which means I get stuck walking home half the third grade on Fridays, and playing with them all afternoon to boot.

As I walk toward the little kids' door, I pass Tricia climbing into her mom's SUV.

"See you at ballet!" Tricia calls.

I've been telling Tricia's mom that Tricia should just walk home with Manuel and me on weekdays, but her mom never goes for that plan. Still, it would make sense. Tricia and I are going to the same ballet class later anyway. But her parents think she'll get more homework done if she goes home before, and they want her to have a healthy snack. It's sort of surprising because my mom's a performing arts teacher, but she doesn't care that much about healthy snacks. She says everyone at her house has to have a full helping of black beans and rice every night, but other than that we're allowed to have whatever we want when we get home from school, and she buys a ton of snacks. That's part of how Manuel got to be so popular: all the third graders have to do is casually mention that Crispy Puffs are their new favorite treat, and my mom will load up on them. Because sugar is Cuba's main crop and she and my dad come from Cuba, she claims that sugar won't hurt us. I don't think that is strictly true (Tricia's grandparents on her dad's side were Cuban too, and her family definitely doesn't say that), but I'm not complaining. Except I think I might have more luck with Tricia's mom if we ate more vegetables after school. The way things are now, Tricia is only allowed to have playdates on Saturdays. I sigh and wave back at Tricia just as the third graders burst out of the door.

CHAPTER TWO

I don't run into Laurita Sánchez until Friday afternoon, when I'm walking home with Manuel, along with his best friends, Eva and Jonah, for, you guessed it, a playdate. Eva and Jonah are twins, which is kind of funny because Eva is tiny for her age and Jonah is a head taller than everyone else in the third grade. They are equal trouble, though—they like to climb, jump, and flip, and they once broke all three of the porcelain ballerinas my mom kept on the mantel. But my mom just said, "Más se perdió en la guerra"—which means that people lost more stuff in some old war in Cuba, so it's not a big deal—and swept up the pieces. You would never have guessed how much she loved those statues. She just asked me to bring the dustpan, put a framed photo of Yolanda, her best friend in Cuba, in the empty space on the mantel, and kept buying Eva and Jonah their favorite Choco Chunks.

"I love having this photo here," my mom says every time

she walks by the mantel. "I miss Yolanda so much, and now I get to see her every day."

The photo isn't very good. It's of Yolanda with her teenage son, Álvaro, and they're both backlit. You can see their matching smiles and Álvaro's floppy black hair that reminds me of Manuel, and not much else. But to hear my mom talk about it, breaking those statues and getting to put up their picture was a lottery win.

The good part about how my mom always says "Más se perdió en la guerra" is that she never gets mad. The bad part is that Manuel's friends never learn a lesson, so if I don't want them to break *my* stuff with their flipping and climbing, I have to keep an eye on them.

A train rumbles by with a loud whistle as I walk Manuel and Eva and Jonah back to our house. Our town, Pine Hill, is only thirty minutes from New York City, and a lot of people's parents take the train to go work there every day. I like that our house is so close to everything: right near our school, the train station, and Main Street. Tricia lives on the other side of town, in Pine Hill Heights. The houses there are bigger and more spread out, and it's too far for her to go anywhere without a ride from her mom. My family can walk to a lot of places, like the grocery store and the pizza place.

We're turning onto our block when I see Laurita heading toward her house from the other direction. Everyone at school calls her Laura, but since her mom's name is Laura too, my mom calls her Laurita so we know that she's talking about the younger of the two Lauras across the street. I guess it's a good system, because I got used to calling her Laurita, even at school, where no one else does.

Laurita has a mitt in one hand and a ball in the other, which she keeps throwing to herself and catching. We cross paths with her just as she reaches her house. She's chewing bubble gum super loudly.

"Hey," I say.

Laurita tosses her ball and mitt onto her lawn and fishes something out of her backpack. It's a stack of flyers, which she tucks under one arm while she pulls out a big roll of masking tape.

"Here," she says, shoving half the stack into my arms. "You can help."

"What? Why?" Laurita must have printed these flyers at school. They're on the blue copy paper that Mr. Fallon buys when we run out of the white printer paper Mrs. Kalinack puts in our classroom. The flyers say BUILD ACORN CORNERS! with a long paragraph about how we need more apartments in Pine Hill.

Laurita rips the masking tape like it's a quiz she failed, then slams a flyer onto the nearest tree. "Because," she says, "you're just standing there, and this is important."

"Okay, fine." I pull a piece of masking tape off *neatly* and put up another flyer a few steps down. I don't think it'll help

Laurita if people see her flyers looking all sloppy. I keep one eye on Manuel and Eva and Jonah, who are jumping over the sidewalk cracks a few steps ahead of us.

Once Laurita sees I'm helping, she finally says, "I guess we have to talk about the committee."

"When do you want to meet?"

"Whenever, as long as it doesn't interfere with softball. Travel this year."

"It can't interfere with ballet, either!" Laurita talks about softball like it's the most important activity there is. It's not like the rest of us don't have stuff to do after school too.

"Oh, right. *The Nutcracker.*"

There's something in Laurita's tone that bugs me, like she thinks *The Nutcracker* is babyish.

"I'm going to be in Party Scene this year." I don't actually know that, but it sounds impressive. "It's a big part."

Laurita blows an enormous bubble that pops in her face. "Sure," she says, like it doesn't really matter. "How about Wednesdays after my softball practice?"

A part of me wants to say I have a super-important rehearsal or something then, but I'm actually free after ballet class. "What time?"

"We just have to be done by seven-fifteen because that's when I call my abuela."

Weirdly punctual, I think, but I say okay. Manuel tugs on my sleeve. "Can we go now? We've been standing here forever!" He knows better than to try to cross the street without me, but that doesn't mean he can stop Eva and Jonah from trying to shinny up a telephone pole, which is what they're doing.

"Seriously?!" I pull Eva down, because she's the smallest and easiest to grab, and thankfully Jonah hops right down after her and doesn't break any bones on the way. I've gotten all three of the little kids across the street before I remember that Laurita and I didn't exactly finish our conversation. I glance over my shoulder and see that she's all the way up the block now, sticking her flyers on every tree and telephone pole.

We roll the third graders' wheelie backpacks up the driveway to the back of the house. As we're turning into our backyard, a little voice pipes up from over the fence.

"Acosta Accordion: smallest setting!"

I flash Davy a thumbs-up, and he salutes back at me. Davy is our four-year-old next-door neighbor. He makes a pretty good lookout because he only goes to a half-day preschool, so the rest of the day he's playing in the yard, where it's easy to keep an eye on who is going and coming up the driveway. I've trained Davy to give me a status report as soon as I come home from school. He calls our house the Acosta Accordion because sometimes it's just my family, like an accordion smooshed to the smallest setting. Sometimes the accordion expands and we have my parents' friends or relatives or a million of Manuel's and Regina's friends over. That's the biggest setting.

"Medium setting now," Davy adds, seeing Eva and Jonah, who make silly faces at him through the fence. He giggles.

Davy holds out his arms, and I lift him over the fence and into our yard. His mom waves at me from their back porch. She loves it when he comes over, which is basically every day. She says it gives her a break. Davy thinks our house is exciting because there are always so many people to talk to. For a four-year-old, he likes to have serious conversations.

"Your mom and dad are inside cooking," Davy announces as soon as he's in our yard. He scrambles to our back door, pumping his chubby toddler arms. I open the door, and Davy jumps across the threshold. "Carmen!" he shouts to my mom.

I hold the door open for Eva, Jonah, and Manuel, who shoots me a glare as he walks inside. Manuel can't stand it when Davy comes over, because Davy likes to play with him and his friends but can't really keep up with their games. Appealing to my mom doesn't help. She sticks with her "Everyone is always welcome" line and tells Manuel to play something else.

In the kitchen, my mom is swinging Davy around. When she sees us, she sets him down and gathers all four of us—Manuel, Eva, Jonah, and me—into an enormous hug. We don't really fit, and my head bumps Eva's.

"¡Mis amores!" She kisses each of us in turn, leaving big red lipstick marks on all of our cheeks. You would think my mom had just come home from a ten-day business trip or something, but that's the way she says hello to everyone. When we come home, she acts like she hasn't seen us in years, like we're sailors who have been away at sea instead of kids who were just two blocks over at school.

I wipe my lipstick smudge off, but Eva and Jonah run up to Davy and press their cheeks to him, leaving a big red second-hand lipstick mark on each of *his* cheeks. He squeals and runs in the other direction, straight past my dad, who is standing at the stove adding crushed garlic to a pot of black beans. Eva and Jonah take off, chasing Davy. My dad tries to get Manuel to stop and say hi to him, but Manuel is two steps behind Eva and Jonah. I guess he's okay with Davy when there's chasing involved.

"Sofía," my dad calls from the stove, "¿y tu papá? ¿Estoy pintado en la pared?"

I grin and go kiss my dad.

"Así se hace," he says happily. "Don't be a scoundrel and ignore your dad like Manuel."

My parents take hellos a little more seriously than other people's parents. They let us invite over whoever we want, but I can tell it bothers them when kids don't pay attention to them.

I love Friday afternoons at my house. The kitchen smells

like garlic and bay leaves, and when there are black beans on the stove, which is basically all the time, it's warm and steamy in here. My mom complains about how old the kitchen is, and how the squares of the linoleum floor keep popping up and getting filled with crud, but it's my favorite room in the house (after the bedroom Regina and I share, of course). Since my parents are performing arts teachers at the high school, my mom is usually wearing black character shoes and a long black practice skirt. I love how the colors of her red polka-dotted apron pop against her black skirt, and how the character shoes look like they're for a fancy party, even though they're really for dance.

"What's new?" my mom asks as she wipes down the counters.

The good smells and kisses made me almost forget Mr. Fallon's party. "Ma, Mrs. Kalinack put me on the History and Contexts Committee with Laurita Sánchez!"

"¡Ay, qué bueno!"

"Are you kidding me? I was supposed to be with Tricia on Decorations!"

My mom waves her hand gracefully, as if she has a magic wand in her hand to wash away all my problems, which she doesn't. "Don't worry about it! You'll see Tricia at *Nutcracker* rehearsals!"

"Auditions in a week!" Papi says. He's chopping a red bell pepper into the smallest pieces you can imagine. "You kids must be excited. *Pum-pa-ra-ra-rum-pum-pum-pum-pum.*" He and my mom start dancing the March from Party Scene in *The Nutcracker*, right there in their aprons.

I lean on the counter. "I was thinking maybe Mrs. Jansen would let me add some new lace trim to the Party Scene dresses; the costumes are getting a little shabby—"

Both my parents stop dancing.

"Mi cielo." My dad comes over and ruffles my hair. "You have to wait for the audition before you get your hopes up. I remember when I was dancing with the Ballet Nacional de Cuba in La Habana—"

I pull away. Manuel and Eva and Jonah will never let me live it down if I end up with garlic and pepper in my hair, and I'm not in the mood for one of my parents' Cuba stories. "I know I have to wait for the auditions, but Regina was a Party Scene girl when she was in fifth grade, and I *am* an Acosta."

My parents look at each other and my mom says, "Well, maybe you and Regina can practice a little before the audition."

I chew the inside of my cheek. I don't really love practicing with Regina. She's a thousand times stricter than Mrs. Jansen and she gets exasperated every time I do even the teeniest step wrong.

"Sofía," my dad lectures, "it's important to work *hard* as a dancer. Tú sabes. When your mami and I were ballet students, everyone wanted to get a great part in every show. But it was only the people who practiced and didn't take things for granted who became professional dancers."

"And if it weren't for that, would we have made it all the way to New York?" my mom says with a wink.

"I *know* I have to work hard," I grumble, but my parents are looking at me with the extra-serious concern of two performing arts teachers. "I'll go get the mail," I say.

My dad goes back to chopping. No one is acting like I'm a long-lost sailor coming home from sea anymore.

I let myself out the back door and grab the mail. I stand out there and flip through everything. Bills for my parents, a *Dance Magazine* for Regina and me, and the bulletin for American Ballet Theatre. I slide my finger under the clear seal so I can look at the bulletin by myself. My whole family always fights over who gets to look at it first, so it's smart to take my peek out here. ABT is my parents' favorite company, and all Regina wants in the world is to dance with them someday. I turn to the centerfold, where they usually announce the biggest performances of the season. There's a glossy picture and a headline across both pages:

BALLET NACIONAL DE CUBA
TOGETHER WITH
AMERICAN BALLET THEATRE
TO PERFORM A SPECIAL TRIBUTE TO
ALICIA ALONSO IN NEW YORK

Then it says:

> This will be the Ballet Nacional de Cuba's first
> performance in the United States in over a decade.
> The two companies will perform a joint program
> on December 20.

But it's the picture below the headline that makes my jaw drop. It's a male ballet dancer with black curly hair in a soaring leap, and I know exactly who it is. I would recognize that face anywhere: his photo is on our mantel. It's Álvaro Ruiz, my mom's best friend's son. Except in this photo, Álvaro is all grown up—and a big ballet star, too.

CHAPTER THREE

"¡Al combate, corred, bayameses!"

I wish this were a joke, but my dad wakes Regina and me up every morning by singing the Cuban national anthem as he climbs the stairs to the second floor. It's a war song, and it's not pretty at 6:30 a.m. on weekdays. It's not pretty at 9 a.m. on Saturdays, either, especially if you have a teenage sister. I've actually been awake for a while, but I still dive under the pillows and cover my ears when my dad reaches the top of the steps.

"¡Que morir por la patria es vivir—*pa-pa-pa-PAM!*"

That last part is about dying for your country, and my dad likes to sound the final drumbeat by pounding it on our door. Like I said, not pretty.

Regina groans and rolls over so that her butt is in the air. She sleeps in the weirdest positions. I'm giggling under the pillows as my dad pushes open the door. My dad leaps in my direction and pretends to sit on my pillows.

"Papi! You're going to squish me!"

"¿Aquí hay alguien?" He acts shocked and jumps off the bed. I poke my head out.

"Yes, and you know there is. Go wake up Regina—she's the one who's still asleep."

Regina groans. "I'm up, okay, I'm up!"

"Time to get ready for ballet class."

Regina slaps her hand to her forehead and slumps back down in bed. "I still have to sew ribbons on my new pointe shoes."

I jump up and head to the closet for her ballet bag. "I'll do it." I'm pretty good at sewing, and Regina is terrible. It takes her forever, and I know she needs time to break in her pointe shoes before auditions next week. She's probably going to get a great part, even though she's only thirteen. Regina's a ballet prodigy.

"Thanks," Regina says.

"And to show her how grateful you are, you'll help your little sister practice?" my dad prompts. I wish he wouldn't. Regina better have a very *long* ballet career, because if she had a dance school, she would be the strictest teacher ever and all of her students would be afraid of her.

Regina looks me up and down, and I stop with my hand on the closet doorknob.

"You want Party Scene?"

I nod. The girls in Party Scene get to wear old-fashioned

dresses with real petticoats and pantaloons, and the parent volunteers curl ribbons into their hair. Regina still has the pictures all over her side of the room of when she and her friends were in Party Scene. Now it's my turn.

Regina sighs. "Just bring your knees *up* on the upbeats and *down* on the downbeats during the March. It's not that hard."

Easy for her to say. She was born with perfect rhythm. Like everyone else in my family. Even Manuel—give him a spoon and he can play an entire drum solo on the kitchen table. I, on the other hand, am always one step behind. It doesn't matter how many times my dad tries to teach me about upbeats and downbeats, it all sounds like music to me. On cue, my dad gets up and starts marching in place, singing the music. He exaggerates his legs coming *down* with a big nod of his head, but I still don't get it.

"All right, Papi, we're awake now." I put both hands on my dad's back and he follows my push, marching toward the door. We look like silly train cars.

"Wait!" Regina says. "I need my phone!"

Still marching, my dad pulls Regina's phone out of his pocket and tosses it her way. She misses spectacularly, but I dive back and catch it just in time.

"Give me that!" Regina shrieks as my dad marches all the way out the door and down the stairs, still singing out beats from *The Nutcracker.*

"Okay, okay, calm down." I hand Regina her phone. No

use throwing things to her. "I'm doing your pointe shoes, re-member?"

Regina's already typing in her password, which is S-O-F-I-A. When I get a phone, I'm going to make the pass-word R-E-G-I-N-A. Unless that's too many letters.

She lowers her phone, which is a big gesture coming from Regina. My parents make her hand it in at nine o'clock every night, and when she gets it back in the mornings, it's like a major event. She needs a solid half hour to catch up. "You're a lifesaver. It would take me all day to sew those ribbons on and I need all the time I can get to break them in."

I salute. "You can count on me."

"Someday when we're on tour with American Ballet The-atre together, I'll make it up to you. I'll buy you peppermint ice cream everywhere we go. I'll make the Metropolitan Opera House get peppermint ice cream in their cafeteria."

I grin. The Metropolitan Opera House is the theater in New York City where ABT has their performances. (I know it's confusing because it's called an opera house, but actually they have a lot of ballets there too.) And I love peppermint ice cream—the real old-fashioned kind, pink with candy bits in it, not the mint-chocolate-chip stuff most ice cream parlors have—but it's hard to find. Regina always has an eye out for places that have it, even though she doesn't like it herself.

"You probably have to know the difference between a downbeat and an upbeat to be in ABT," I say.

Regina is back to her phone already, but she raises an eyebrow. "So get practicing, girl."

I will, I tell myself. But first I have some sewing to do. I double-check that our door is all the way closed and that Manuel and his friends are nowhere in sight. I can hear them playing out in the yard. Good. You can't do anything private in our house unless you double-check that Manuel and his crew are far, far away.

In the closet, I tug on the lightbulb string and close the door behind me. It's not that big a closet; there's just a row of hangers and a few shelves on either side. The ones on the left are for Regina, and they are the weirdest closet shelves in the history of shelving. They are full of neatly stacked shrink-wrapped packages. She has a brand-new bead kit, a musical jewelry box, and a dance skirt in a set with matching leg warmers, all sitting there in their original packaging. It looks like she robbed a toy store. Actually, it's because her birthday is in January, right after Christmas, so she *stockpiles* her gifts. Every year after we've all torn open our presents, Regina plays with one thing, then puts the rest away. Sure, she'll rip off the wrapping paper, but she won't take anything out of its packaging. She does the same thing on her birthday, and by Reyes on January sixth, she's got a nice little stash of unopened gifts. She puts them in our closet, and every month she takes out a new present for herself. My parents think it's clever and charming, but it's actually infuriating. For example, there is no way Regina is going to sit around and make necklaces with the super-deluxe bead kit our tía Rosi got her for her birthday last year. She'll get bored and walk away before it's finished. I don't know what Tía Rosi was even thinking buying it for her—I'm the one who likes crafts in this family. I could really use the glass beads in the kit as trimming for a costume I'm working on, and Regina usually shares, but I can't get her to even *open* the darn thing. Living with my sister can be complicated.

I grab Regina's ballet bag off the closet floor, then scan my side of the closet. My shelves look like everyone else's, with clothing and books shoved in the corners. I find my sewing kit, then carefully move a stack of T-shirts to the right so they hide the cardboard shoe box I've been storing behind my sewing things. I'll bring that box down to the basement later.

"Sofía, are you playing in there again?" Regina yanks open the door and I whirl around quickly.

"What's it to you where I play?" I check that the T-shirts are in place.

"You are so *weird*," Regina complains, ushering me out into the bedroom. For someone who is getting free pointe shoe sewing this morning, Regina sure is grumpy. I used to hang out and read and do crafts on the shoe bench beneath the hanging clothing. It was the perfect place, where no one bothered me. But I don't really fit anymore, and Regina always said I was being a vampire and should get some actual sunlight, so I stopped.

While Regina catches up on her phone, I thread a needle with dental floss and start sewing ribbons onto her pointe shoes. People are always surprised that I use dental floss, but it holds much stronger than thread, and when a dancer is whirling around the stage, the last thing you want is a ribbon popping off. Out of the corner of my eye, I watch Regina. I can almost tell by the movements of her fingers that she's about to open Instagram.

I didn't feel like telling my family about what I saw in the ABT bulletin when I opened it on the porch yesterday. Seeing Álvaro in that big glossy picture looking like a famous ballet dancer and not like my family friend sort of bothered me. It's like there's a way things are supposed to be: my mom smiling at that photo on the mantelpiece, telling stories about Yolanda when they were kids, complaining how she wishes she could see Álvaro grow up. Glossy-photo Álvaro just doesn't fit. So I stuffed the brochure into my backpack and didn't show it to anyone. My family is going to find out eventually—probably any second now, since Regina obsessively follows ABT dancers on Instagram—

"Oh. My. GOD!" Regina yells.

I should buy lottery tickets. I might as well be a fortune-teller; that's how well I can predict Regina's Instagram habits.

"MAMI! PAPI!" Regina yanks open the door and waves

her phone around in the air as she runs down the stairs. I scramble to my feet and follow her, a pointe shoe and a half-sewn ribbon still in my left hand.

"¿Qué pasó?" My mom meets Regina at the landing, her face wrinkled with worry. My dad isn't far behind.

Silently, Regina hands over her phone. The same picture of Álvaro, the one from the ad in the bulletin, shines on her screen. "Read the caption!" Regina urges.

My mom puts her finger down to scroll, but she's too slow. Regina's phone locks on her.

"Sofía! Sofía!" Regina yells, and my mom looks up at me, startled. "No, it's the *password!*" Regina shouts, grabbing the phone from my mom and typing it in herself. She scrolls to the caption and gives it back to my mom.

My parents' faces are both still and focused as they read. Then suddenly everyone is jumping up and down and screaming, and my mom is running for her cell phone and my dad is running for his and they're both yelling about how no one even told them and who was the company bringing and what kind of party are we going to throw and what are the exact dates. I sit down right there on the bottom of the stairs and finish sewing Regina's pointe shoe.

My parents start calling people immediately. They get through to Yolanda in Cuba, who tells them the plans. Yolanda is too old to dance professionally anymore. Like my mom, she teaches dance now, but not at a high school. Instead,

26

she teaches the students at the school of the Ballet Nacional de Cuba.

"So is she coming?" Regina urges my mom to ask. "They have to bring her!"

"Sí, claro," my mom says, listening intently to Yolanda's voice on the other end of the line, then filling us in. "They're bringing Yolanda to help the dancers prepare for the big show."

Then a huge smile spreads over my mom's face, and she repeats "¡Felicidades!" and "¡Enhorabuena!" into the phone over and over again, congratulating Yolanda. When she hangs up, my mom tells us that Álvaro, who is only seventeen, has been selected to perform a solo.

Regina gasps. We met Álvaro the last time we visited Cuba, but I had no idea he was that good at ballet now. The Ballet Nacional de Cuba and American Ballet Theatre are both a pretty big deal. If Álvaro got a solo for their joint performance in New York City, he must be one of the best.

My parents make plans to have Yolanda and Álvaro come stay at our house during their trip to New York, which is going to be almost three months long, because Álvaro will be doing some other performances before the big show at the Metropolitan Opera House. While my parents are still on the phone, a dreamy look comes over Regina's face. She closes her eyes and hums the tune to the ballet *Theme and Variations* and begins dancing around the kitchen. Of all the weird things Regina does, this is the weirdest. She likes dancing with her eyes closed, because Alicia Alonso, the Cuban *prima ballerina assoluta* (this means "extra-extremely-really-you-should-have-heard-about-her-by-now famous"), began to lose her sight when she was young and did some of her most famous dancing when she was nearly blind. My sister says Alicia Alonso was really able to *feel* the music, so now she practices with her eyes closed. It's one thing for Alicia Alonso, who didn't have a choice, but I think my sister is going to break an arm dancing around the kitchen like that. Plus, I don't like *Theme and Variations.* I don't get why my sister is always practicing it. There's no story in the whole ballet. It's just a bunch of people dancing. There's no villain, no happy ending, and no set. Why would anyone want to watch it? But try telling Regina that while she's pirouetting around the kitchen, eyes closed.

Sometimes I think it must be nice to be in Regina's head, where there's one present every month, and everything is ballet and Alicia, and the beats are always perfectly in sync.

CHAPTER FOUR

"I think you're getting the hang of it, Sofía!"

It's Saturday, which means Tricia could come over. We're in my living room, where the furniture is pretty much permanently pushed back to the edges so people can practice dancing in there. Every time my parents have a party, we remember that most people don't keep their carpets rolled up in the corner and the couch and chairs piled against one wall, and we have to rearrange everything before guests arrive. But today it's perfect, because Tricia and I have lots of room to practice.

"I watched the video of last year's performance," she explains. "So I know the March from Party Scene by heart."

"Wow," I say, impressed.

"I *really* hope I get Party Scene this year," Tricia says. "You're lucky you have Regina to practice with. I wish I had someone to help me."

"Trust me, you do *not* want Regina helping you practice. And anyway, you're so good already you don't need help." I'm the one we have to worry about.

"There's another dance in Party Scene too," Tricia goes on. "It's called the Grandfather Dance."

I know that, but I nod like Tricia said something really enlightening. It's awkward to tell someone, "I already know basically everything about dance because I'm an Acosta." It makes you sound snooty, even if you're not. But I don't really want to learn the Grandfather Dance now. It's supposed to be a funny dance because the grandfather character busts out and does a hilarious jig in the middle of the stage, but the grown-up who plays the grandfather doesn't come to rehearsals, and kids still have to do a serious dance. Plus, the Grandfather Dance is at the very end of Party Scene. It's a long scene—definitely longer than any other part I've had in *The Nutcracker* before—because it's made up of lots of different dances, with acting in between. The audience is supposed to feel like they're at a real Christmas party. It's hard to imagine Christmas in September, but Mrs. Jansen says December sneaks up on you real fast if you don't start *Nutcracker* practices early.

But still, it's ages away. "I think I'm okay," I say quickly. "I feel ready for the audition. Want to go down to the basement?"

"Sure."

I breathe a sigh of relief. Because Tricia only really gets to come over on Saturdays, we have to make the most of the time. We stop in the kitchen, where Tricia helps herself to a Chewy Bar. My mom keeps them in the cabinet just for Tricia.

No one else in my family eats them, but my mom wants all of our friends to have at least one snack they *really* like in our house.

I'm holding open the basement door when Manuel zooms into the kitchen and through the door.

"Thanks!" he shouts back at me as he careens down the steps to the basement.

"I wasn't holding it open for you!" I shout back. Actually, what on earth is Manuel doing in the basement? I run down after him. Tricia follows more slowly, still munching on her Chewy Bar.

The basement is unfinished, with concrete floors and low wooden rafters in the ceiling. There are plastic bins for winter clothes and Christmas decorations, and the porch furniture for the summer. My mom has thrown white sheets over everything to keep the dust out, which makes it looks like creepy ghosts, not seasonal storage. Our basement would be a great set for a Halloween movie.

"Manuel?" I ask. He's randomly pulling sheets off things. I raise my voice. "I don't think you should be touching Mami and Papi's stuff!"

He shakes his head. "I'm looking for a sled."

I stare at him. "Manuel. It's September. There's no snow."

The words are barely out of my mouth when Eva and Jonah charge past me.

"Did you find it?" Eva starts tearing sheets off things at

a record pace. There's a chandelier on the floor now. Upside down, it looks like the underbelly of a sparkling jellyfish.

Tricia sidles up next to me. "Don't they ever go *home*?"

I throw my hands up. "Apparently not."

There's a galloping sound on the stairs above us, and then Davy appears, his little round face glowing. "Your dad said I could come over! What are we doing? Sheet-pulling?" He grabs a sheet from Jonah and they start a tug-of-war. Of course Davy is going to lose because Jonah is twice his size, so I intercept them.

"EVERYONE STOP!" I holler.

Manuel, Eva, Jonah, and Davy all freeze. Even Tricia raises an eyebrow at me.

"Put down the sheet," I say calmly.

Jonah and Davy lower the sheet to the floor. Davy's mouth is in the shape of a perfect O. I guess he's not used to people yelling at him in the Acosta household.

"It is September," I tell the little kids in what I hope is a mature, commanding voice. "You cannot go sledding. You cannot take the sheets off Mami and Papi's stuff. You have to go play outside."

Eva puts her hands on her hips. "Who put you in charge, Sofía Acosta?"

"My parents, actually. And I say upstairs." I jerk my thumb at the basement stairs.

Huffily, Eva leads the way to the staircase. When Manuel,

Jonah, and Davy are lined up behind her, Manuel biting his lip and Davy still looking terrified, she shoots me a withering glare over her shoulder and sticks her tongue out. Then she marches up the stairs, looking like the world's teeniest mother duck with her overgrown ducklings.

Tricia and I throw the sheets back over the furniture. "Your basement is so organized. Mine is full of all the junk we don't use anymore."

Which is funny, because the rest of Tricia's house looks like a photo shoot for an expensive catalog. I shrug.

"You know how my parents are. They think keeping stuff we've outgrown is like a high crime." Stop playing with a toy or wearing an outfit for one week and my parents will donate it to the church faster than you can say "Más se perdió en la guerra"—which is what my parents will say if you complain, along with a nice lecture about a giving spirit, so no one ever complains. But that's where the basement comes in handy.

Tricia follows me past the storage piles to the corner beneath the staircase. The area is blocked off by the boiler, so no one ever comes this way. But if you slip past the boiler, there's a space the size of a walk-in closet.

This is my hiding spot. I have a whole collection of stuff here: a basket of Beanie Babies, three plastic baby dolls plus their cribs and strollers, a row of Barbies, and my three stuffed animals, Mr. Rumpkins, Solarie, and Jingle. Mr. Rumpkins is a teddy bear who wears a yellow raincoat, Solarie is a hippo in a tutu and sunglasses, and Jingle is a plush green emoji who jingles like a rattle when you shake him. Don't ask me how I know Jingle is a he, because I just do. Maybe he told me when I was a little kid.

Tricia is the only person in the world who knows about this spot. Everything here was supposed to go to the church at some point, but sometimes I squirrel stuff away before my parents drop off the donation bags. I know that's not really right and there are kids who don't have any toys, and I know I'm technically too old for Barbies and stuffed animals, but I just don't believe that any other kid would love my stuffed animals as much as I do. They might not know that Jingle is a boy, or that Mr. Rumpkins wears his raincoat even when it's not raining because he just likes how the plastic feels. Those are important facts about them. Besides, if Regina is allowed to have a closet full of brand-new stuff she never even touches, why can't I have a spot for old stuff that I use all the time? I *need* all these Barbies for my sewing.

I have a whole vision for sprucing up the Party Scene dresses at ballet, and I've been practicing by making mini versions of the dresses for my Barbies. I've been using whatever trimmings I can find in our house and working on them when no one is around. Now I take a finished doll out of my pocket. I had been hiding her in the closet behind my old T-shirts while I worked on her, but now I line her up with the other Party Scene girls (Barbies) and see how the colors go together.

"They look so good!" Tricia claps her hands excitedly. "I hope Mrs. Jansen lets you add those trimmings to the real thing—they're so sparkly and perfect."

"I wanted them to look as good as *The Nutcracker* at Lincoln Center, but still be ours." A lot of ballet schools want everything they do to be exactly like the big *Nutcracker* that's performed at Lincoln Center in New York City—the one with the flying sleigh and the forty-foot-tall Christmas tree. I *love* the costumes and the set for that version of *The Nutcracker,* but it wouldn't be original if ours looked exactly like that one. Still, the Party Scene dresses for our ballet school have been used for many, many years. The dress Regina wore three years ago is beautiful and I was so jealous of her when she wore it, but I took a look at it in the costume closet last week and it barely has any lace left on it. So I need to do something before Tricia and I end up in laceless dresses.

I turn the Barbie doll to show Tricia her headpiece, which is made of lace with teeny-tiny paper flowers.

"How did you make the flowers so small?" Tricia breathes.

"It took me forever. I had to borrow an X-Acto knife from my dad to cut the paper."

"He let you?"

"I lied and said it was for a present I wanted to make for Yolanda, my mom's friend who's coming to visit from Cuba. He knows I'll be careful. But look." I pry apart a little corner of one of the flowers with my fingernails so Tricia can see how I dropped tiny jewels of glitter glue into the centers. "Just enough sparkle to catch the light."

"You're so good at this stuff, Sofía. I wish I had your talent."

I smile widely. "You're really good at a lot of stuff! Like remembering all the steps in Party Scene."

Now Tricia is blushing. I throw my arms around her. Having a best friend is *the* best. "I just can't *wait* until we're both Party Scene girls. We'll get to use the older kids' dressing room at the theater this year!"

Tricia squirms. "We still have to get the parts. And there are two months of rehearsals before we even get to the theater!"

"I know." I shrug. "But I just have that feeling. Like it's all going to be perfect."

Tricia fingers the headpiece I made. I can tell she really likes it. I'm going to use her favorite colors, lavender and daisy yellow, when I make her headpiece for Party Scene. She'll be so excited when she sees it.

"I was thinking," Tricia says slowly. "Well, Stella and I were thinking, about the Decorations Committee—"

"Yes?" I've been thinking about it too. Even though I wasn't assigned to the committee at school, I can still help with the outside-of-school stuff, kind of like an honorary member.

Tricia takes a deep breath. "We thought the Decorations Committee members should wear special outfits to Mr. Fallon's party."

"Oh?" Somehow I'm getting the feeling this isn't about my becoming an honorary member.

"I told Stella how good you are at making headpieces, and we thought you could help us make red-white-and-blue barrettes for us to wear. Abdul and Lucas are making red-white-and-blue wristbands, and Stella and I wanted something for our hair, too."

"Like for everyone in the class?"

Tricia frowns. "No, just for Stella and me."

"Yeah," I say, trying to sound offhand. "No problem. Just tell me what you want and I'll make them for you."

Tricia squeals. "You're the best! I can't wait to tell Stella."

I duck my head and adjust Mr. Rumpkins's raincoat so that Tricia can't see my face.

CHAPTER FIVE

"We got it!! We got Party Scene!!!" I shout to the sky as Tricia and I run outside.

Mrs. Jansen's Ballet Academy, which is the name of our ballet school, is on the first floor of an office building on the edge of town. There's a high stoop with seven steps to get into the building, and UPS and FedEx drop boxes are lined up next to the stoop. In the summer, you can sit on the top of the boxes and swing your legs down. Regina says the kids who do that might fall and are jeopardizing their dance careers. I say Regina doesn't know how to live. But right now, I'm not thinking about summer. All I'm thinking about is the parent information packet I'm waving in the air. Underneath a bunch of stuff about what a big commitment it is to perform in *The Nutcracker* and how there will be a zillion rehearsals, the packet says:

YOUR CHILD HAS BEEN CAST IN THE ROLE OF: *Party Scene Girl #3.*

It's written in blue ink, in Mrs. Jansen's own messy handwriting, so I know it's real. And Tricia's says *Party Scene Girl #2*. We are going to be in Party Scene! We're going to stand next to each other in most of the dances. We can pretend to be best friends on the stage, just like we're best friends in real life. I even asked Mrs. Jansen whether I could help the parent volunteers with the costumes, and her mouth twitched a little, but she didn't say no. This is what my dad would call being in business.

I run down the stoop to meet my parents in the parking lot. They're both standing outside the car, talking to Jessie and Mike's mom, Mrs. Lewis. Mike is my sister's age and one of the only boys in the advanced class, and Jessie is younger than Manuel. She's a little kid who will probably play a Baby Mouse or an Angel. I don't talk to Mike and Jessie much, because they're not my age and they don't go to my school—they live in East Bolton, which is a different school district—but I like Mrs. Lewis. She's usually in charge of measuring people for costumes, and she helps some of the other parents make the alterations and repairs that need to be done every year. I should talk to her about my idea for the Party Scene dresses.

"Sofía!" Tricia shouts across the parking lot. She's standing three cars over, outside her mom's SUV. They're parked next to a bunch of other parents from our school, and everyone seems to be hugging their kids and patting them on the back about their roles. I run over and say hi to Tricia's mom, Mrs.

Rivera, who is wearing black capris and a silk blouse. She's tall like Tricia, and her purse is so tiny it's hard to believe she can even fit car keys in there.

"I heard the good news," Mrs. Rivera says with a wink at me, slipping her phone into her teeny purse. I swear it's like a Houdini act. "We're going to have a lot of car pools this fall, I bet."

Another parent laughs and shakes her head. "Tell me about it."

"And have you heard about this girl's mom?" Mrs. Rivera says, pointing to me. "She has guests coming for three months! Can you imagine? In the middle of all of this."

I guess Tricia told her mom about Yolanda and Álvaro.

The other mom puts her hand to her heart. "Oh my gosh, I can't imagine." She looks down at me like it was all my idea. *Three months?* Then she turns back to Mrs. Rivera. "Having a house guest for longer than four nights is asking for punishment!"

"I know," Mrs. Rivera laughs. "But you know the Acostas."

Tricia and I are mostly ignoring the grown-ups talking while we pretend to be Party Scene girls, but I turn around when I hear that.

"What about us?" I ask curiously.

Mrs. Rivera pats my back. "Oh, you know how your mom is. Always having strangers over."

I open my mouth to say that Yolanda and Álvaro aren't

strangers, since Yolanda and my mom have been best friends since they were my age, but before I can get to it, Mrs. Rivera beeps open the door to her SUV.

"Dad's making dinner," she says to Tricia. "Time to get going. Give your mom a kiss for me, okay, Sof?"

I nod, wishing I could actually get a minute to talk to Tricia and her mom about Yolanda and Álvaro's visit, but everyone is already piling into their cars. I realize that I haven't even told my parents that I got cast in Party Scene. I dash back across the parking lot to our car.

My mom is promising to pray for Mrs. Lewis's sister, who is in the hospital. Mrs. Lewis's family lives in Jamaica, so she hasn't been able to visit.

"That must be so hard," my mom says, fishing in her shoulder bag for an estampita. She's constantly giving people these little cards with her favorite prayer and a picture of a flower on them. She keeps tons of them in her bag, which is always full of snacks, makeup, hairspray, and superglue for pointe shoe emergencies. The problem is that the prayer estampitas are the same size as the estampitas they give out at people's funerals, and my mom doesn't always pay attention. This can get awkward. I double-check that my mom is giving Mrs. Lewis the right card before waving the parent information packet in my mom's face.

"Look!!! Party Scene!!!"

Mrs. Lewis is the first to see. "All right, Sofía! You're going to be great, honey!" She gives me and each of my parents a hug before getting into her car, where Mike and Jessie are already strapped in.

"¡Mi amor! ¡Qué maravilla!" My mom and dad both shout and smile and hug me, and I'm grinning ear to ear. I can't believe they thought there was even a chance I wouldn't get Party Scene. Basically everyone in Level 5, which is my ballet class, is going to be in Party Scene, except for Zaria, who is too tall and is going to be in a different part of the show instead.

Regina and Manuel are the last people to come out. Regina is deep in conversation with Mrs. Jansen, who's locking up the studio. Manuel is swinging his arms and whistling.

"Soak those feet in the hottest water you can stand," Mrs. Jansen is telling Regina. "They'll be good as new tomorrow." Mrs. Jansen straightens up. She has short hair that's dyed reddish brown, with just a little bit of gray roots showing. She always wears the same black sequined jacket and black boots with a heel. She's tall, but she doesn't look much like a ballet dancer anymore. She doesn't wear her hair in buns or ponytails like my mom. If you just caught a glimpse of her, you would think she was like every other old lady. But when she walks, you know. She was a dancer. Her hair and eyes and skin are all so different from my mom's, but they move exactly the same: like they're floating. Regina, too. She glides to our car.

I keep talking about Party Scene until Manuel kicks the back of the front passenger seat. "Hey. Doesn't anyone want to know what I'm going to be?"

I roll my eyes. "You're going to be Fritz, just like last year." Fritz is the little brother character in *The Nutcracker*. He's supposed to be pesky. Unfortunately, you have to be a pretty good dancer to be Fritz, and there aren't as many boys at our ballet school as girls, and none of them are Acostas but Manuel. So he was Fritz last year, even though he was only seven, and everyone told him how amazing and talented he was and what a wonder it was that he could perform like that at such a young age. I think it went to his head.

"I could have any part," Manuel says defensively.

"Let me guess, is it"—I pretend I'm thinking hard—"Fritz?"

My dad clears his throat. "Manuel, cuéntanos. What part did they give you?"

Manuel glares at me. "Fritz."

My parents coo and shout over him like it's some kind of accomplishment, and to make things worse, Manuel adds, eyes on me, "So this will be my *second* year in Party Scene."

I decide to ignore him.

"Regina, what are you? Are you going to be in Snow and Flowers again?" Last year Regina wowed everyone by being the first seventh grader to be in both the Waltz of the Snowflakes and the Waltz of the Flowers, which are hard dances that take place on pointe. Usually only high schoolers are in them, but like I said, Regina is a ballet genius.

"Um, yeah. I'm going to be in Flowers again."

There's something in Regina's tone that makes me turn around and look at her. She's sitting in the way backseat, with her feet stretched out in front of her and her ankles neatly crossed. Regina's skin is lighter than mine, so you can tell, for example, when she's gone a little pale, or when she's blushing. She's the only one in my family whose skin changes color like that. Right now, her cheeks are pink.

"What?" she says, turning pinker.

"Give me that." I reach my arm back and grab the packet she's holding in her lap.

"No, I don't want to tell—"

My jaw drops. "*Dewdrop?* You're going to be *Dewdrop?* That's like the second-biggest part in the whole show!" Dewdrop is the lead in the Waltz of the Flowers, flitting between all the other dancers (the flowers), pretending to be a drop of morning dew.

At the traffic light, my dad turns around to get a good look at Regina. "Mi reina—" And then he doesn't say anything else. It's like Regina has left us all speechless.

My mom takes the packet from me. "Estos papeles son para los papás," she says, grumbling that we didn't give her our parent information packets as soon as we got in the car. She studies the words on Regina's packet and bites her lip.

Usually, Mrs. Jansen gets teenagers from the School of American Ballet, a serious dance school in New York City, to dance the lead roles in our shows. She pays them and everything. Most of them go on to be professional dancers, sometimes only a year or two after they perform with us. We always have five teenagers come from SAB to play five roles: Sugarplum, her cavalier, Snow Queen, *her* cavalier, and Dewdrop.

Dewdrop is always someone from SAB in New York City. She is always a high school senior. She is a future star. She is never an eighth grader from Mrs. Jansen's Ballet Academy in Pine Hill, and definitely never my sister, Regina Alicia Acosta.

"So what's for dinner?" Regina asks weakly.

CHAPTER SIX

Tricia and Stella are *very* interested in Regina at school the next day. Before the morning announcements, Stella runs over to where I'm sitting with Tricia and Abdul.

"Sofía, is it *true*? Mrs. Jansen gave your sister *Dewdrop*?"

This is really getting annoying. When we got home from the auditions last night, my parents recovered from their speechlessness and we had to call like six different continents to tell our relatives. You think I'm exaggerating, but Tía Rosi, my mom's sister, lives in Miami, Florida, her other sister, Aldema, lives in San Juan, Puerto Rico, and my dad's brother, Leonardo, lives in Cuernavaca, Mexico, and that doesn't even include my mom's friends and family in Cuba, who we usually message instead of call. So I guess that's not really six continents, but it's *a lot* of different places, and you get pretty sick of hearing my mom tell the same story again and again. My mom is so loud when she's excited that even in the basement I can still hear every word she's saying. She didn't tell a single person that I got into Party Scene. Everything was about how Regina is going to be Dewdrop. Apparently Mrs. Jansen told Regina she is showing "great promise"—which is not exactly news, I could have told you that—and that she wants her to audition for ABT's very exclusive summer intensive program. She can use her Dewdrop performance for her audition videos. My mom had to make sure the whole of Latin America heard this non-news individually, from her.

"It's true," I tell Tricia and Stella, pulling out my marbled notebook. There's already a Do Now journal prompt on the board, and we're supposed to be working on it.

"Wow," Stella says breathlessly. "Is it because your mom helps out with the show?"

My neck practically snaps up. "What? No, of course not! It's because Regina's the best ballet dancer north of Cuba—everybody knows that."

"She is *really* good," Tricia jumps in.

"Yeah." Stella nods knowingly. "She's the best in the advanced class, and she's probably the youngest in the group."

"Everyone else in the advanced class is in high school, Stella." I don't really know why Stella is over by our table. She didn't hang out so much with Tricia last year. She had other friends at school, and even though she's in our grade, she was a level behind us at ballet until this year, when she somehow zoomed into our level.

The morning announcements crackle over the PA system, and Mr. Fallon motions for Stella to go back to her seat.

Mr. Fallon is the best teacher at our elementary school.

We start every day with a Do Now. Sometimes people write really hilarious things, like when the prompt was about an alien army taking over our school. Mr. Fallon also wears silly ties, and Thursday is officially Ugly Tie Day in his calendar. Once he wore a tie with a picture of Mrs. Kalinack's face on it for Ugly Tie Day. It's amazing she still wants to throw him a surprise party. Except I get it. Mr. Fallon might make fun of Mrs. Kalinack, but I've also seen him bringing trays of coffee to the main office and laughing with her when it's his turn to help with the bus line. He's just that kind of person.

The prompt today is to write a story about what would happen if school closed for the day and we could do whatever we wanted. I get started right away. We only have twenty minutes for journaling time, and I have a ton of ideas. The first thing I would do is call Tricia and ask for a weekday playdate. Her mom would say yes, of course, because this is a fictional story. We wouldn't have any homework. I write about how we would make an entire set of new costumes for the *Nutcracker* characters. Everyone would be totally wowed by our work and throw us a huge party to celebrate. Regina's friends from middle school would come and everything.

My hand is the first one up when Mr. Fallon asks if anyone wants to share their story. I practically jump out of my seat, but Stella's hand is faster. I slump back while she reads a boring story about going to play tennis with friends at the country club and then jumping in the pool. I've been to the country club a few times, because Tricia is a member. It's not that fun. There are all sorts of rules and lanes at the pool. If you want a good pool, you have to go to my aunt Aldema's house in Puerto Rico. She lets everyone do whatever they want in it, and she owns just about every floatie ever invented.

There's a loud sigh in the back of the room, and we all turn to where Laurita is sitting, at an island of three desks with Lucas and Jayden.

"Laura, is there something you wanted to say?" Mr. Fallon's eyebrows are raised. His eyebrows are bushy and orange, just like his hair and beard and mustache. Usually Mr. Fallon is smiling and making jokes, but there's nothing funny about his expression today. It's a why-aren't-you-listening-respectfully expression.

Laurita crosses her arms. "Yeah. I think country clubs are snooty and racist."

Lucas giggles. This is typical Laurita. She's always talking about things that are snooty or racist or bad for the planet— last year Tricia and I named her the Bad News Machine because she got on everyone's case about recycling until our fourth-grade teacher convinced the PTA to buy our whole school new bins.

Stella looks like she got caught in the middle of an intersection with the red hand flashing and doesn't know where to turn. "Um, well, anyone is welcome. My mom has guest passes, so you could come sometime, Laura—"

Laurita rolls her eyes and huffs.

I wriggle in my seat. I've never really thought about country clubs before, other than to rank their pools. I glance at Tricia and she's also giggling nervously, sort of like Lucas. She raises her shoulders when I catch her eye, as if to say, "I don't know what to do either; this is awkward!"

Finally Mr. Fallon cuts in. "Could you tell us why you think that, Laura?" He adjusts the stool he's sitting on, like he doesn't see fifty eyeballs looking at him and wondering what he's thinking. You never let Laurita get started. She'll just go on and on.

"Well," Laurita says, sitting up in her chair. "Country clubs used to exclude people. When my neighbor Mrs. Miceli moved to Pine Hill, she wasn't even allowed to join the country club, because she's Italian. Same thing was true for other immigrants, and people of color."

I didn't know that about Mrs. Miceli. She's like a zillion years old and never goes outside, so I don't know when Laurita talked to her.

Tricia cuts in testily. "It's not like that anymore, Laura. Two of my grandparents were Cuban, and we're members."

But my *parents* are Cuban, and we're not. I wonder if there's something to what Laurita is saying, even today.

"I'm half Italian," Stella says faintly. She's still standing there holding her notebook. Someone should give the poor girl a break and tell her to sit down.

"Yeah, now they don't care who you are, as long as you're rich." There's something bitter and nasty about Laurita's tone, and for a second the hairs on the back of my neck stand up, almost like I'm at a scary movie, except I'm not. I'm sitting in Mr. Fallon's class. It's the class we've been waiting for all through elementary school, and I have the seat next to my best friend. I don't know why my neck is behaving this way.

"That's not fair!" Tricia raises her hand and waves it until Mr. Fallon calls on her, even though she already talked out of turn. "My dad works hard so we can afford the country club. Just because other people don't work as hard doesn't mean Laura should be jealous."

"I'm not jealous!" Laurita bursts out. "But lots of people work hard and still can't be members of your useless club."

"Why is she so mean?" Tricia whispers to me, covering her mouth with her hand so Mr. Fallon can't hear.

Jayden mutters, just loudly enough for the people sitting near him to hear, "Who would want to be in a club with *Laura* anyway?" I press my pencil to my paper, making a dark gray circle in the corner of my notebook. Stella sits down, staring at her hands.

It's like we're frozen, and no one knows what to do next. Then Lucas starts giggling, and Mr. Fallon asks, "Lucas, how about you share your journal entry?"

"*Snap*," Jayden says, and everyone laughs, because we all know Lucas has written approximately two words in the entire twenty minutes. Even Lucas himself laughs, shrugging and spreading out his palms like he's saying "Guilty," and Mr. Fallon changes the subject to math.

When I bend down to get my math workbook from my desk cubby, I can see the back of the room, and I notice Laurita wiping her eyes. Laurita's so tough, always chewing gum and pounding her softball mitt, that it surprises me. But then I think about what Jayden said. Anyone would cry. I almost go over to Laurita to say something nice, but Mr. Fallon is already loading up our math lesson.

I turn to Tricia. At least I can help my best friend, who still looks pretty hurt that Laurita called her club useless. "What did you write about?"

Tricia shrugs. "Same as everyone—having a day off would be cool." She shuts her notebook, but not before I catch a glimpse of her entry.

Tennis with Stella is written at the top of the page, with lots of words below in her neat and tiny handwriting.

"What about you?" Tricia asks.

"Nothing," I say quickly. I slam my notebook shut. Now that I see what Tricia wrote, I don't want to tell her about the weekday playdate I imagined for us, or the party at Mrs. Jansen's. I just want to do math.

That night when Regina and I are in bed, I ask her about it.

"Do you think it's bad to be a member of a country club?"

Regina snorts. "I wouldn't worry about it."

"Why not? Laurita Sánchez says they're racist and snooty."

"Whatever they are, I don't think there's much chance of us becoming members, Sofía."

I think about this. "You mean because we go to Puerto Rico every summer? They do stuff at the country club in the winter, too. Tricia and her mom go to all these lunches and things—"

"How on earth would Mami and Papi afford to be members of a country club? Do you have any idea how expensive our house is?"

Nope, I have no idea. I've always lived in this house. My parents moved here after Regina was born but before I was. I've always shared this room with Regina. My bed has always been against the left-hand wall and her bed has always been perpendicular to the right-hand wall. There's always been a painting of a girl in a boat with the words TE REGALO UNA ESTRELLA hanging over my bed, and a picture of my parents in a performance of *Coppélia* in Cuba hanging over Regina's bed. My mom has always sat on my bed when she reads to us at night, even when she squishes me. I never thought that much about how much it all cost.

"It's a lot of money, Sofía. Like, *a ton* of money. Mami and Papi want us to live in Pine Hill so we can go to school here, but it's expensive. And food for all five of us plus all of Mami and Papi's guests plus pointe shoes for me every month adds up. Next year you'll be on pointe too, and that will be even more money."

I've heard my dad make jokes about how much pointe shoes for Regina cost, but my mom always shushes him. Ballerinas need new pointe shoes every few weeks to support their feet. There's no way Regina is ever getting to American Ballet Theatre if my parents don't spring for the pointe shoes.

I feel wriggly again, so I snuggle down under the covers and try to think of cozy things, like the smell of my parents' black beans and how cute Mr. Rumpkins looks in his yellow raincoat. I wish he were here in bed with me, instead of down in the basement.

"But we'll be okay, right, Regina?" It's scary to think about my family not being able to afford things.

I might as well be talking to the air. Regina is humming the tune to *Theme and Variations*. Just enough light from the streetlamps gets into our room for me to see her outline in the darkness; her head is moving rhythmically from left to right, and I know she's lost again, dreaming of dance.

CHAPTER SEVEN

Yolanda and Álvaro are arriving next week, so my mom spends the weekend cleaning the house. Álvaro's going to sleep in Manuel's room, and Yolanda is getting the attic, which is tiny and has a slanty ceiling. Manuel and I use the attic all the time, but grown-ups don't usually like it because it's easy to bang your head on the way down the stairs.

When Tricia comes over on Saturday, we head straight down to the basement so we can get away from my mom, who is dragging whoever she can into helping her sort bedding and fold towels. Luckily, she's so distracted that she won't notice Tricia and me disappearing for a while.

Behind the boiler, I tell Tricia about an idea I had to make a cardboard theater for our Party Scene dolls and decorate the set. Jingle, Solarie, and Mr. Rumpkins could be the audience. As soon as Tricia hears, she starts unloading supplies out of her backpack.

"My mom gave me some broken costume jewelry," she

says, pulling out a crushed-velvet pouch. She spills the little bag of rhinestones and silvery chains onto the piece of cardboard I'm using as the stage. "Maybe they could be decorations for around the curtains?"

"Ooooh, great idea!" I reach for a bottle of glue I keep in the basement. "It'll look like the Pine Hill Playhouse." That's where Mrs. Jansen's Ballet Academy performs *The Nutcracker*. It's an old-fashioned Victorian theater. Silhouettes of women with parasols and petticoats decorate the walls, and around the curtains are gilded curlicues and carvings of soaring angels. I want my cardboard theater to be that elaborate, so Tricia's jewels will be perfect. After I cut the cardboard frame, we glue them all around the edges.

"We did awesome!" Tricia proclaims when we're done.

"We could probably be professional set designers," I agree.

Just then, the basement steps creak. Tricia and I lock eyes. It's definitely not Manuel, who always runs and whose steps are small and light. By the sound of it, this is a grown-up. We freeze in place while the footsteps go right by our hiding spot. The staircase sags a little with each step, so the boards almost touch the heads of Solarie, Jingle, and Mr. Rumpkins. Finally the footsteps pass, and I hear my mom humming *Nutcracker* music in front of the laundry machine on the other side of the basement.

"You know the drill," I whisper, and we duck out from behind the boiler and make our way slowly around to the other side of the basement. With any luck we can head back up-stairs without my mom noticing.

"Pero niña, ¿tú qué haces aquí?"

Busted.

"Nada," I lie. "Just, um, looking for something I lost."

My mom raises an eyebrow.

"Hey!" I point to the laundry basket at her feet. "That's not clothing!" The basket is full of crayons, scissors, faded construction paper, a handful of Disney figurines, and one of my very favorite baby dolls—one that actually plonks out plastic poop emojis when you sit her on the toilet. We lost the toilet that came with her a long time ago, but the doll is still pretty funny.

"I'm taking these to church," my mom says. "There's no space for Yolanda with all the junk you and Manuel have in the attic!"

I groan, and above us the door to the basement opens. Regina's footsteps are light and dainty, and her back is perfectly straight as she hands my mom another basket of used art supplies. "What are you two doing down here?"

"Mami's getting rid of my stuff!" I hate how high-pitched and babyish my voice sounds, but I can't help it.

My mom sets down the basket. "Ay, Sofía, no seas así."

"She's right," Regina says. "Don't be selfish. Besides"—she picks up the baby doll—"this thing is gross. Do we really need to keep it?"

"Verdad," my mom agrees, snatching the doll back from Regina and dropping it in the basket. "Yolanda and Álvaro need a comfortable place to stay. The ballet is barely giving them enough money for the trip, and New York is so expensive. The attic needs to be clean."

I open my mouth to complain again, but Regina puts her hands on her hips. I *hate* when she acts like she's my mom's vice president or something. "Sofía, how would you feel if you went to stay in another country and your friend's lousy kid wouldn't even get rid of some old junk?"

I swallow hard and say nothing as my mom picks up the basket and heads to the door on the other side of the basement.

Regina marches upstairs, and I turn back to Tricia. "I'm not selfish, I just don't think my stuff is the problem!"

"Sure," Tricia says.

"I could have moved it all to my room," I grumble. "What do your parents do when people visit?" I ask before I remember what her mom said about not having people stay for a long time.

Tricia shrugs. "We have a guest room."

Right. Tricia's house is so big that even if her mom did invite someone for three months, they wouldn't have to get rid of anything. Then I have a thought.

"What about your dad? Has anyone his family knew in Cuba ever visited?" Tricia's grandparents were from Cuba, so maybe her dad still knows people there. She's never mentioned it, but then again, it's not like I talk about Yolanda and Álvaro all the time.

"Umm, I don't think so?" Tricia shifts her feet awkwardly. "It's been a long time since my grandparents moved here. We're just Americans now."

Which is an odd thing to say, because I don't think knowing people in Cuba has anything to do with being American or not. My mom's always telling me how it's so great that Tricia and I are both Latinas, like it's this special thing we have in common. But I don't think Tricia sees it that way.

Before I can say anything else, Tricia smiles mischievously and opens her hand.

My mouth drops. It's one of the figurines that was in the basket: my favorite Disney princess, Ariel, in my favorite one of her dresses, a pink ballgown. Perfect for Party Scene inspiration. Tricia hands me the figurine and throws her arm around my shoulder. As we head up the stairs, I hold the Ariel figurine tightly in my hand, and Tricia's words melt away.

CHAPTER EIGHT

"Hola, señora Acosta," Laurita says, kissing my mom's cheek. She sure is polite when talking to a grown-up. No slamming flyers or calling clubs useless around my mom, I guess.

My mom laughs and pulls Laurita into a one-armed hug. "Laurita, you should call me Carmen," she insists. In Pine Hill, kids call adults Ms. or Mr., as if all the grown-ups were teachers. My mom thinks it's silly and tells everyone to call her by her first name.

My mom asks Laurita if she's staying for dinner, but Laurita shakes her head. "Tengo que estar en casa a las siete y cuarto."

My mom nods. "Of course, that's when you call your abuelita. I forgot."

Before I can ask my mom how she knows everything that's happening in all of Pine Hill, she sashays off to the living room to help Regina practice Dewdrop. Laurita and I troop upstairs.

We sit on the floor of my bedroom, and Laurita pulls out a spiral notebook. She's all business.

"People at Mr. Fallon's party need to know why being a citizen is important. That's what our exhibit should be about."

"Maybe we should make a poster explaining what a citizen is. With all the responsibilities and rights Mrs. Kalinack was telling us about."

Laurita nods. "And how hard it is for immigrants who *don't* get to be citizens."

"We could make the poster in the shape of a big heart," I say. "With outlines of people in it. And it could say that becoming a citizen is like . . ." I think for a second. "Like becoming a part of a family! It means you always belong no matter what—"

"—but you have to help the people in that family, too," Laurita adds. "And sometimes your family isn't that great."

"I have an idea! We could use puff paint on the posters to make them stand out!"

Laurita taps her notebook. "We have to plan out the information first. We might need to go to the library for research."

I groan. It's like my committee assignment is an extra book report.

Laurita ignores me and moves right along. "We should include all the stuff from the immigration unit at school."

We've barely started the immigration unit. So far Mr. Fallon just asked us to find out where our families were from. Laurita is so extra.

"But *personally,*" Laurita goes on, "I think we need at least one section on Acorn Corners."

"What's Acorn Corners?"

Laurita raises an eyebrow. "You don't remember? You helped me hang the flyers!"

I search my memory. "The apartment building?"

"Of course the apartment building! It's really hard for immigrants to find a place to live when they come to the United States, so when Acorn Corners is built, it will help them."

"Doesn't Mr. Fallon already have an apartment?" I don't think other people are going to be as excited about Acorn Corners as Laurita is.

She shakes her head. "Yeah, but lots of other immigrants don't. My Titi O has like a two-hour bus ride to work because she can't afford somewhere close to the city. It's not that easy to live in Pine Hill, you know."

I remember what Regina said about how expensive it is. "I know that," I say.

"Plus, lots of grown-ups talk about diversity, but they never do anything. If they build Acorn Corners, there could be more different colors and races living here."

"My mom would like that. She's always joking that she sticks out in Pine Hill because there aren't more Latinas, like her—but it might just be because no one else does ballet steps up and down the grocery aisles."

Laurita throws back her head to laugh. "After they build Acorn Corners, we'll get your mom a dance buddy." She takes her watch off her wrist and puts it on the floor where she can see it better. "I have to make sure I'm not late."

"Okay." Then I ask curiously, "Why do you always call your abuelita at exactly seven-fifteen?"

"That's when las señoras leave. The women who take care of her. She lives in the Dominican Republic all by herself, and if we don't call, she gets sad. She sits by the phone and waits for us."

I look down at my hands. "My mom's friend Yolanda and her son, Álvaro, are staying with us for a whole three months," I say. I'm not sure what this has to do with Laurita's abuelita, but I want to tell her. "To make room for them, I had to get rid of some of my . . . stuff." I almost said "dolls" but I could imagine the look on Laurita's face, so I changed it.

Laurita nods. "When my family comes from the DR, I'm stuck on the couch the whole time."

I think of all the puff paint waiting in my closet, and all the brads and rhinestones I was saving up for the Decorations Committee. I sigh. Then I ask, "Are there going to be any bulldozers or cranes when they build Acorn Corners?"

"Yeah, they're building it in that old parking lot by the grocery store. Haven't you seen the banner on the fence? There's a picture of what it will look like when it's built."

"Manuel will like that. He's still really into construction trucks. I'll take him to see it." I smile at Laurita. "And I'll do some research for the exhibit while I'm there."

At the top of her notebook page, Laurita has written

EXHIBIT SECTIONS in all caps. Now she takes out her pencil, and on the first line below it, she writes: *Acorn Corners: Sofía.*

"You know, there are only two of us—we can probably remember who got assigned to what," I say, still smiling.

Laurita gives me a stern look. I shut up fast, but it makes me giggle, too. There's something so funny about serious Laurita.

"I've gotta go now," she says. "Abuelita time."

I stop giggling right away. "I'll walk you home."

"It's right across the street," Laurita says, gathering up her stuff.

"Still."

Outside, Laurita puts her hands in her pockets. We look both ways.

"Remember the other day? When we talked about country clubs in school?"

"Yeah?" Laurita says defensively.

"I'm sorry people were mean to you. Especially Jayden."

Laurita snorts. "Now you're sorry. You just sat there while Jayden was talking."

"I didn't mean to! It's that Tricia really likes the country club, so I didn't want to hurt her feelings either."

Now that I say it aloud, it wasn't a very good reason for letting everyone be mean.

"I should have stuck up for you. Sometimes—I don't know, I'm so worried about people being mad that I don't say anything."

We're almost at Laurita's house now, and she drags her feet. "I know. I'm like that too. It's not fun when people tell me I'm annoying or whatever."

"I thought you didn't care what *anyone* said. Except that day, I guess—I—well, I saw you cry."

"They hurt my feelings," Laurita says simply. We get to her house and she stops on the sidewalk in front. "Thanks for walking me. You didn't have to."

I smile. "You know how it is. I was just sitting there, and this is important."

CHAPTER NINE

My mom, Regina, Manuel, and I are all in the kitchen.
Regina is practicing the arm movements from Dewdrop while
Manuel does little *jetés* around the kitchen. I'm folding a napkin into a teeny-tiny crane. We're all a little nervous. My dad
left to pick up Yolanda and Álvaro from the airport a while
ago, and they should be here any minute.

When my dad's minivan pulls into the driveway, we run
outside. Everyone is shouting and kissing. My mom and
Yolanda are clinging to each other and laughing and there are
tears running down my mom's cheeks. Álvaro is making the
rounds, kissing everyone and slapping their backs heartily.

My mom and Yolanda are the same age. Yolanda's skin is
wrinkled from sunlight, but her body is all energy. Her face
is wide and full of laughter, and her steps are light and ener-
getic. I can tell she's a dancer too, but she's less dreamy and
romantic than Regina or even my mom. She's vivacious. So is
Álvaro. His hair reminds me of Manuel's: curly, floppy, and

held back by a headband. But Álvaro is tall and handsome. When he gets to me, he kisses my cheek and says, "Sofía Carmen, ¡cuánto tiempo!"

"Yeah," I reply.

We stand there for a minute, and then Yolanda swoops in and scoops me into a hug. I smile nervously. It's weird, seeing Yolanda and Álvaro here, in our driveway. Even though my mom talks about Yolanda all the time and keeps her photo on our mantel, I've only ever met her once before, when my parents took us on a trip to Cuba two years ago. I watch the door of our minivan close automatically when my dad presses a button on the key fob, and I remember that when we were in Cuba, Yolanda called a friend to pick us up, because she doesn't have a car. The car her friend came in didn't have seat belts. Manuel had to sit in my mom's lap instead of a car seat, and there was definitely no automatic sliding door. Álvaro and Yolanda have only been here a few minutes, but every time I look at them, I get a guilty, nagging feeling.

It's like this: I can act a lot of different ways. I'm one way when I'm teasing Regina and another way when I'm helping Manuel. When Tricia and I are doing crafts in the basement, I'm different than when I'm trying to practice at ballet. The last time we saw Álvaro and Yolanda, it was in Cuba, and I knew how to act then. I spoke to them in Spanish and I ate the food they made and I didn't wear a seat belt. But now Yolanda and Álvaro are standing in our driveway, and I don't know whether to be Cuba Sofía or Pine Hill Sofía. I'm torn. I don't know why—I speak Spanish with my parents all the time, but not usually to other kids, so it feels awkward with Álvaro. My mind goes to Fruit Roll-Ups. Would Álvaro think I was spoiled if I went and got one right now? Because suddenly all I can think of is how I want to eat a Fruit Roll-Up and hide.

Instead, everyone settles into the living room, and I sit perched on the edge of the couch. Manuel is curled up in the corner, working on a Rubik's Cube and ignoring everyone, which no one seems to mind because he's just a little kid. But I think I have to pay attention. My mom and Yolanda are telling each other stories they both know by heart about when they were growing up in Cuba, and Regina is hanging on Álvaro's every word. He's telling her about ballet competitions he's done all over the world. He won a medal at a youth dance competition in Paris. Regina looks ready to jump up and start practicing right then and there.

"Did you ever get to meet Alicia Alonso?" Regina asks breathlessly, in Spanish. She doesn't seem to have language-choice-confusion paralysis like I do. I swear she could learn a language on the spot if it meant she got to talk about ballet.

"Sí, claro," Álvaro replies. "She was always around the ballet school."

"Wow."

"After my dad left," Álvaro goes on, "my mom and I spent a lot of time there."

"What happened to your dad?" I blurt out in English.

Álvaro cocks his head to the side for a second, but I guess he understands me, because he answers, "¿No sabes? He moved to Switzerland when I was a little kid. He got a job with a ballet company there." Álvaro shrugs. "Haven't heard from him since."

"Oh." That's sad. No one told me. I kick the couch with my heels, back and forth. Then I have a thought. "Does that mean he and Yolanda are divorced now?"

Álvaro laughs, then leans toward me. "They were never married," he says, lowering his voice. "But yeah, I wouldn't mention him around my mom."

Regina shoots me a stop-asking-personal-questions look, but Álvaro winks at me. I smile back. Maybe it will be fun having a teenager other than my sister around.

"I can't believe you're going to get to dance on the stage of the Metropolitan Opera House," Regina goes on. "You'll get to go to rehearsals at the ABT studios and everything!"

Álvaro grins. "Maybe I can sneak you backstage. And Sofía."

Regina might faint from excitement, so I reply quickly, "Regina's the dancer, not me." I don't even know why I said that, except that Álvaro is an international-award-winning ballet dancer and it seems weird to compare myself to him and Regina.

"Really?" Álvaro asks. But he says it like it's no big deal. "What do you like to do, then?"

I think for a minute, picturing the cardboard theater and Barbie-doll costumes in the basement. "I like to sew, I guess."

Yolanda turns to face me. "¿Oí a alguien hablar de costura?"

"Mamá," Álvaro says, "Sofía's a seamstress, like you."

I am not exactly a seamstress, but I do know how to sew. Yolanda smiles delightedly and asks me if it's true, so I lift my shoulders and put my hands between my knees as if to say, "I guess so."

"Well," Yolanda goes on in Spanish. "I want to go to the fabric shops in New York City one day while we're here. I'd like to get a few things to make for Álvaro and the other dancers. You'll come with me!"

My mom gushes about what a great idea this is, and she and Yolanda go back to talking to each other, leaving me with Regina and Álvaro.

"Maybe someday," Regina says to Álvaro, "we'll both be in American Ballet Theatre *together*. Wouldn't that be an incredible tribute to Alicia? It would be like a full circle—she was part of the very beginning of ABT and all these years later Cuban ballet dancers are still joining ABT."

Yolanda frowns and stops talking to my mom to listen. Regina says this all the time—about following in Alicia's footsteps to ABT—and people usually smile indulgently at her when she says it. Instead, Yolanda is wrinkling her brow.

"Álvaro is going to join the Ballet Nacional de Cuba when he graduates," Yolanda cuts in. "It's nearly arranged already."

Álvaro stares at his hands and doesn't say anything. Regina looks back and forth between the two of them, then smiles brightly. "Well, that's a great company too!"

"The Ballet Nacional de Cuba was very important to Alicia," Yolanda says, a little stiffly. "After the 1960s, she poured her whole heart into it."

I wriggle in my seat, trying not to look anyone in the eye. The 1960s are when Cuba became a communist country, and my family talks about it all the time. Communism is a type of government that tries to make everyone equal so that everyone can have enough food and clothing, go to the doctor, and get an education—that's the good part. The bad part is that communism doesn't usually work, and Cuba is still a poor country. The United States government *hates* communism, so since the 1960s, the United States has had an embargo on Cuba. That means that people in the United States can't travel to Cuba easily and can't buy things from Cuba. The United States thought if they made things super difficult, Cuba would give up on being communist. But mostly, the embargo just makes everything harder. It stinks.

After the 1960s, it wasn't easy to go back and forth between Cuba and the United States. There's the embargo, and the Cuban government makes it hard for people to go in and out of Cuba too. Alicia Alonso had to pick a country to live in permanently, and she picked her homeland, Cuba. But I wonder if she wanted to make a choice at all—if it wouldn't have been better if she could have kept dancing in both the places that mattered to her. If my mom had a choice, I know she would want to see Yolanda more than once every couple of years.

My mom claps her hands together and changes the subject to something less awkward. "Okay then, how about lunch? Everyone must be hungry." She hurries into the kitchen and starts pulling dishes out of the cabinet. I go and help her. Through the glass door in the kitchen, we see Eva and Jonah waving. Davy is looking eagerly through the bars in the fence.

"¡Me cachi en diez!" my mom shouts, seeing them. "I forgot I told Manuel he could have Eva and Jonah over." She calls for Manuel and opens the door. "Eva, Jonah," she says brightly, putting one hand on each of their shoulders and steering them toward the living room, "you have to meet our friends, Yolanda and Álvaro." She introduces them, and then Manuel drags his friends away. I go back to the kitchen to keep setting the table. My mom seems to have gotten lost in a conversation in the living room again, but I know how she likes to do things and I put out all the place settings.

The back door in the kitchen is a little bit open, but I leave it. I like the cold air; the kitchen is hot from my mom cooking all morning. I hear Manuel and Eva and Jonah running around outside. Manuel is telling them about how Álvaro is going to be sleeping in his room.

"Then where are you sleeping?" Jonah asks.

"The floor, of course."

Eva giggles. "The *floor*? You're always sleeping on the floor. That's where my dog sleeps!"

"Manuel the puppy!" Jonah shouts, and Eva and Jonah start barking. Davy joins in from the other side of the fence. I toss the dish towel onto the counter and go outside. The first thing I do is lift Davy over the fence. It's really not fair for Manuel and his friends to be out there with Davy just desperate to join in and not invite him. Then I turn around and see Manuel, Eva, and Jonah scrambling up a big rock near the side of our garage.

"What are you *doing*?" I ask.

"Going up to the garage roof!" Manuel yells.

"Are you out of your mind?" I grab Manuel and pull him down from the rock. I guess I'm a little rough, because he bumps his arm.

"Ow!" he screams. "Sofía, leave us alone!"

"Yeah," Eva complains. "We were having a good time before you came out here."

I can't believe Eva. "Actually, you were trying to break your necks before I came out here, *and* making fun of my little brother. Do that again and . . ."

Eva raises an eyebrow. I have no idea what to say.

"And I'll . . ."

She taps her foot.

"Well, you'll be in trouble," I finish finally. "Just knock it off."

Eva smiles sweetly, but as I head back into the house, I

hear all the kids making barking noises. Davy doesn't know better; he just thinks they're playing dogs. But there's something about it that bothers me. It's *nice* that Manuel is giving Álvaro his bed for a few months. Álvaro is seventeen and dancing in a major ballet performance in New York City—he needs a comfortable place to sleep. Manuel is eight and falls asleep anywhere. I hate how Eva makes it seem like Manuel sleeping on the floor is something lowly and pathetic.

I stomp back inside and overhear Regina telling Yolanda and Álvaro about being cast as Dewdrop in *The Nutcracker*.

"Mijita, how wonderful," Yolanda is saying. "You'll see, your talent will give you many opportunities. Wherever you go, people will open their doors because of your abilities."

I plop down on a kitchen chair. Until Regina got Dewdrop, I had never really thought about whether *I* had talent. I'm an Acosta; that should be enough. But now I wonder if someone would sleep on the floor to make space for me if I ever went to another country. Or do doors only open for people who become Dewdrop when they're just thirteen?

CHAPTER TEN

"Remember to smile! It's Christmas Eve and you're at a party!"

It's not actually Christmas Eve, it's the second Saturday in October, but *Nutcracker* rehearsals are in full swing. Mrs. Jansen is busy in the small studio with Regina, giving her a private lesson, so Sharon, who used to be one of my mom's students at the high school and is now going to community college, is running the Party Scene rehearsal.

Here's the thing about Party Scene. You're supposed to *look* like you're at a Christmas party having the time of your life, but it's a lot of work. You have to be in specific places at specific times or the whole scene falls apart, and there's a lot to remember.

The story of *The Nutcracker* starts at a Christmas Eve party that a girl named Clara and her little brother, Fritz (played by Manuel, of course), are having at their house. All of their friends come—those are the Party Scene boys and girls. There are also parents in Party Scene, but they don't come to our rehearsals until December. They're played by actual parents, including mine. Then Clara gets a nutcracker doll from her godfather, Drosselmeyer, and Fritz breaks the doll, and then Drosselmeyer's nephew, who turns out to be a handsome prince, fixes it for her. This all takes place in Germany more than a hundred years ago, which is why everyone has German names and wears dresses. After Party Scene ends, the nutcracker comes to life, battles the evil mice who are camped out in Clara's living room, and whisks her off to the Land of Sweets. It's a magical land inhabited not by people but by sugary treats who each represent a different part of the world, like Hot Chocolate from Spain and Marzipan from France. They all dance for Clara, and then all the flowers of the land waltz with their Dewdrop (played by Regina). The plot is a little silly, if you ask me, but I do love all the costumes in *The Nutcracker*. When everyone is onstage in the final scene, there's an explosion of color, like the frosting swirl of the world's fanciest cupcake, and all the bows and lace and sequins are like the glittering sprinkles on top.

I think I'm getting the hang of the March. Greg is my partner, and I've known him forever. He goes to school in East Bolton, but he's been in my ballet level since we were little kids. He's pretty good about this whole upbeat-downbeat thing, so as long as I follow what he's doing, it more or less works out.

"Sofía Acosta, you're half a beat behind everyone else!" Sharon calls out. "Listen to the music, please!"

Greg gives me a light shove and I gain some speed to keep up. After forty-five minutes of March, March, March, Sharon finally gives us a break. "Twenty minutes, everyone, then Mrs. Jansen is taking over."

We all let out a whoop. Mrs. Jansen has a habit of running late. Twenty minutes is definitely at least thirty minutes of free time.

As soon as Sharon is out the door, Manuel starts goofing off. He wriggles under a painted marquee from an old set that's shoved in the corner and yanks something out of the prop box beneath it.

"I got something!" he announces, holding up one of the dolls the girls get as gifts during Party Scene.

"Toss it here, little man!" Torrey yells. He's in middle school and is playing the Prince. He always pays a lot of attention to Manuel, like he's his honorary big brother.

Manuel winds up and tosses the doll to Torrey, who catches it in midair. Torrey shouts that the canvas backdrops folded up in the corners are bases, and he runs around them, trying to make it back to the speaker system, which is home.

"Team up, everyone!" I shout, and I join Manuel in the outfield, which is really the side of the studio with the windows and barres. Everyone plays the game, except for Stella. Believe it or not, she's standing at the barre in our outfield *practicing* the March, even though she knows all the steps by heart already.

Manuel catches up to Torrey and jumps on his back. Torrey roars like a lion.

"Gooooooal!" I holler happily as Torrey finally swings Manuel down and winds up to pitch the doll to Carrie, who plays Clara.

After about a zillion tackles and home runs, we all fall into a heap, exhausted.

"Let's get a soda." Carrie tugs on Torrey's leotard, and he agrees in an instant. The rest of us in Level 5 watch them jealously. I'm not allowed to leave Mrs. Jansen's during rehearsal breaks unless Regina is with me. I can't wait until I'm in middle school and can just stroll down to get a soda or candy at the deli whenever we have free time.

Stella is still standing at the barre, going through the steps of the Grandfather Dance. Sharon hasn't even taught it to us yet, but Stella's face is all screwed up like she's concentrating really hard, and I can see her lips silently mouthing out the beat.

I shake my head and get to my feet. "Let's go look at the costumes," I say to Tricia. "We have plenty of time."

"Sharon told us to stay here," Tricia says.

"It's not like we're going outside, just to the costume closet."

Tricia glances at Stella, who still has her focus-pocus face on.

"I should stay and practice," she says.

I march Tricia out the door. "You are already one of the best in Party Scene—you do *not* need more practice."

Tricia laughs, but I see her sneak one more look back at Stella.

I push open the door to the costume closet. The smell in here is the best smell you've ever inhaled. It's fresh-clean hairspray, just-pressed steamer, and the tiniest hint of sweat all mixed together. When I walk in here, it gives me the same thrill as the curtain being pulled aside on opening night. It reminds me how lucky I am to be an Acosta and to dance in performances on real stages with real hair and makeup and lights and costumes. It's even sweeter when I think about how my parents learned some of these same dances in Cuba—I like that ballet is similar no matter what country you're in.

I walk down the rows of costumes toward the Party Scene dresses, which are way at the back. I stop for a minute to check out the Dewdrop costume. It's white and covered in beads and sequins. Regina is supposed to look like a delicate drop of dew, flitting between the flowers. I examine it carefully to make sure none of the beads are coming loose, and that it looks like it will fit Regina. I notice a few missing sequins and try to remember to tell my mom, or ask Mrs. Jansen if I can sew them back on myself. It would be a disaster if Regina's costume wasn't perfect since she's going to use the performance for her audition tapes.

"Yolanda told me she's going to take me to a fabric store

in the city," I tell Tricia. "One of the big stores that has like a thousand different materials and colors."

"That's your mom's friend?"

"Uh, yeah." Even though it's only been a few days, to me it feels like Yolanda and Álvaro have lived with us forever. I forget that Tricia hasn't met them yet.

"Why does she need fabric?" Tricia asks.

I wave my hand at the costumes. "Because New York City has the best fabric stores, so she wants to buy some material to make costumes for Álvaro and the other Cuban dancers. Plus, he needs to look good at rehearsals with ABT. He's going to be dancing at the Metropolitan Opera House, after all!"

"I can't believe you know someone who's going to dance at the Met," Tricia says. "And meet people from ABT!"

I nod proudly. "I bet this summer Regina will meet people from ABT too. She's definitely getting into that summer program." Sometimes having a dance genius for a big sister has its advantages. Like when people are super impressed that you're a ballet insider.

Tricia pulls out Torrey's Prince costume. It has ruffled lace and gold stripes up and down the legs. "He is going to look so dreamy in this," she says.

I wrinkle my nose. "Dreamy? He's going to look more like a cupcake in that thing!"

Tricia giggles and pulls the costume off the hanger. She holds it in front of her. "Scrumptious," she says, smacking her lips together and striking a pose. "Cupcake for sale!"

We both laugh hysterically, and I grab one of the Spanish Hot Chocolate costumes. "Piping hot cocoa, sip me right up!" I holler, and Tricia pretends to slurp from the shoulder while I giggle uncontrollably.

Someone yanks open the closet door. "Sofía Carmen, is that you?"

Tricia straightens up and shoves the Prince costume back onto its hanger.

Regina storms down the aisle. "What are you two *doing* back here? Your rehearsal is starting!"

Tricia bolts like the building is on fire. She hates being late to anything.

"Calm down!" I shout back at Regina, arranging the costume more neatly on its hanger.

"You know you're not supposed to be back here; you and Tricia could have broken something and then you'd be in huge trouble!"

I throw my hands in the air. "For your information, I was checking your costume to make sure it was perfect! I'm the only one in this family who can sew, remember?"

Regina's face is red, and it's like she didn't even hear what I said. "You have to stop goofing off in here and pay attention! You're embarrassing our entire family, Sofía."

"I am not!"

"You are too. People are going to think the Acostas don't work hard—listen, there's the music! Mrs. Jansen probably thinks you're skipping!"

I push past Regina, grumbling as I go. We just wasted another five minutes on this conversation. Regina gets so worked up about every little thing involving ballet.

I rush into the big studio, and sure enough, Mrs. Jansen is marking out the steps to the Grandfather Dance.

Stella shadows Mrs. Jansen's movements carefully. She's sticking out the tip of her tongue just the tiniest bit, as if she's thinking too hard to pay attention to her tongue. It's not very party-like.

Mrs. Jansen's eyebrows shoot up when she sees me. "Sofía Acosta, please take your place."

I try to shadow Mrs. Jansen's movements like Stella. Mrs. Jansen isn't actually demonstrating the whole dance, she's just moving her arms and saying the names of the steps. While she does that, we're all supposed to move our arms like her so we remember the steps. Professional ballet dancers call this marking. But before I know it, Mrs. Jansen is starting up the music and everyone is rushing to their places. The Grandfather Dance is done in pairs, in height order, which means that Manuel and Dahlia are right at the front.

"Beautiful!" Mrs. Jansen praises them. After a few bars of music, she claps for our attention. "Everyone take a look at Manuel and Dahlia. They're not just dancing, they're *acting*— see how well they hold the audience's attention?" She nods to them and turns the music back on.

They're total hams—Manuel bows with a flourish and winks dramatically at the audience. Dahlia pretends to almost faint when Manuel presents her with an imaginary flower. We laugh out loud.

"See?" Mrs. Jansen says. "You have to remember to *act*. This is a party, after all!"

We take it from the top. Greg and I try to make our movements dramatic and big like Manuel and Dahlia's. We end up giggling a lot. Then we get to the more serious part of the dancing, and I have to focus to remember the steps. A few times Greg yanks me in the opposite direction at the last minute. "Not that way," he hisses. "You'll bump into Stella and Zack!"

I peek at them in back of me in the lineup. Stella's not sticking out her tongue anymore; instead, she's smiling. It's a little pasted on but definitely looks more festive than when we were marking.

Looking at Stella got me all distracted, and Greg has to grab my arm again. "Hop-step!" he whispers, and I join in, but now all the steps are muddled in my head. I can't remember what comes after the hop-step, but I think it's sliding and curtsying, so I take a big slide and, *smack,* hit Abdul, who is right in front of me.

"Ow, Sofía!" he whines.

"What, it's just a little bump," I say, trying to figure out where everyone else is in the dance now.

"STOP!" Mrs. Jansen stomps her foot. We all freeze in place. She pauses the music. "Sofía Acosta, *what* is going on?"

Everyone inches away from me. It's like being under a

spotlight, but not a good one. The kind they have at jails for when they interrogate the prisoner.

"Umm—I just got a little mixed up."

"A little mixed up?" Mrs. Jansen does not seem to be joking around. "A *little* mixed up? Sofía Acosta, you've been goofing off, you were late to rehearsal, you didn't follow instructions—" She puts her hand in her dyed hair like she's ready to yank it out just over me. "Your brother and your sister are working hard on this performance, and it's a joke to you, isn't it?"

I stay very still. This is what I do when a bee gets too close to me with its stinger—I play statue so it will fly away.

But it doesn't work with Mrs. Jansen.

"Is this a joke to you, Sofía?"

"No, Mrs. Jansen."

"Then I suggest you start acting like a fifth grader and not a toddler. Everyone else is going to take a five-minute break. When we get back, I expect you to have the Grandfather Dance memorized." Mrs. Jansen glide-walks out of the big studio, the heels of her black boots clip-clapping the floor in perfect rhythm.

All of Party Scene stares at me.

CHAPTER ELEVEN

The day the heat comes on for the first time is the coziest day of the whole year. The radiators make our house and our school and even the inside of our car smell like steam and dust, which I happen to think are delicious scents. My parents worry about dry air and plug in humidifiers. It's raining this morning, and when my dad marches up the stairs singing "¡Al combate, corred, bayameses!" I want to snuggle back under the covers and melt into the warmth. But I get up anyway, because I need to get to school. Today is the next secret planning meeting for Mr. Fallon's surprise party.

Down in the kitchen, I help Manuel into his rain boots and coat so we can get out the door.

"Ay, Sofía, no sabes cuánto te lo agradezco," Mami says, leaning on the kitchen counter. She is so happy when someone else helps Manuel with winter stuff, or really anything involving snaps and buttons. She tells everyone who will listen how the worst part of having kids in the United States is bundling them into winter gear. She claims that factories add so many hooks and loops to winter gear on *purpose*, just to annoy *her*, Carmen Alicia Acosta.

Álvaro is sitting at the kitchen table next to my dad. I guess not all teenagers sleep until the last possible minute like Regina does. He's spreading guava jam on toast, and his ankles are crossed neatly under the table.

"Are you going to help me, too?" he says in Spanish, winking at me. "This is going to be my first winter."

I laugh. "It's only October." I grab Manuel's scarf and loop it twice around his neck, then step back and look at it. I think it would be better a little looser, so I redo it until it's just right.

My mom laughs. "Sofía has an eye for style," she explains to Álvaro.

I don't know why my mom always finds that so surprising. She is super elegant in her black character shoes and swishing practice skirt. It's just that when it comes to outdoor gear, we're more of a mismatched-hand-me-downs kind of family than a matching-L.L.Bean kind. That's why I pay close attention to Manuel. Since I bring him to school, he's like a representative of my dressing abilities. I want him to look sharp.

Yolanda comes in the back door and wriggles off my mom's rain boots. She's carrying four coffees, which she hands out to my mom and dad and Álvaro.

"Took you a long time!" Álvaro pulls the lid off his coffee.

Yolanda shakes her head. "You won't believe what hap-

pened! I was looking for the right change and everyone behind me was in such a *rush*. I said I would just be another
second, and as soon as I opened my mouth, the woman behind me said no wonder I was holding up the line—she said
I didn't even speak English!" Yolanda is flustered and out of
breath as she finishes telling the story.

"But you *do* speak English," I blurt out. Which is true.
Maybe not as well as my parents, but she doesn't have that
much more of an accent.

My mom tsks and shakes her head. "People here can be
awful. I'm going to tell the people at the store the next time
I go in—"

"Oh, please don't," Yolanda says, still looking frazzled. "It
was nothing." She takes a sip of her coffee and sniffs.

My dad claps his hands together. "Just wait until everyone
finds out you're a famous ballet dancer! And that Álvaro will
be performing at the Met! You'll be the most popular family
in Pine Hill."

Yolanda doesn't say anything, but she smiles through her
coffee. I wave at everyone and hurry Manuel out the door.
My dad is probably right. If you're a ballet dancer, people usually end up being nice to you. Yolanda has nothing to worry
about.

I'm the one who's in trouble, I think, remembering the
Nutcracker rehearsal. I hold Manuel's hand extra tight the entire walk to school.

* * *

At lunch, Stella, Tricia, and I talk about decorations for Mr. Fallon's party—the headpieces I'm making them, and how we're going to get enough glitter for the red-white-and-blue flag cutouts they want to make. I'm so into our conversation that I almost forget I'm not on the committee. At least, I forget until Abdul slides onto the bench next to me and asks what Laurita and I have planned so far.

"Oh. It's going to be cool. We're going to use puff paint on the exhibit." I don't know why I'm talking about the puff paint instead of the part of the exhibit Laurita and I actually agreed on. It's just easier to talk to Abdul and Stella and Tricia about paint.

"Maybe you should practice what you're going to do before the meeting," Abdul says. "You know, so you don't bump into me?" He nudges me like he's made the funniest joke of all time, and Tricia bursts into laughter. I scowl at both of them. I don't need to be reminded of my disastrous *Nutcracker* rehearsal.

"I wouldn't have bumped into you if you weren't being so slow," I retort, which isn't true, but it's mean of Abdul to bring it up. He makes a face at me and slides out of our bench. I pick at my sandwich.

"Oh, come on, Sofía, he was just teasing," Tricia says. "He didn't mean anything by it."

I still don't answer, and Tricia's face softens.

"You'll be fine in Party Scene. I'll help you."

Stella jumps in enthusiastically. "Yeah, we definitely will!"

I'm about to be grumpy that Stella thinks she is on the same *we* as Tricia and me, but then she keeps going.

"I know lots of great memorization tricks; my mom and I looked some up online last year"—Stella falters—"you know, when I wasn't in your level yet."

I had practically forgotten that Stella wasn't in our ballet level until this year. It's starting to feel like she was always there, marking the steps with her tongue between her teeth. I almost laugh out loud, thinking of what my mom would say if I started marking that way—something about how Cubans are supposed to dance with ¡alegría! and ¡ánimo!—but then I don't say anything.

"Thanks, you two," I say instead, and I get busy chewing on my sandwich: bologna with too much mayonnaise, because my mom is really terrible at sandwich-making. Luckily, she makes up for her terrible sandwiches by packing really good treats. I fish around for the Twix bar that's in the bottom of my lunch bag and automatically snap off a piece for Tricia, whose mom always packs her a bento box. It's like a work of art, with carrot shavings and broccoli florets arranged in patterns, but absolutely zero dessert. Tricia nibbles at her piece of my Twix bar neatly, around the edges. She's never told her mom that she's actually had a piece of dessert every single day of elementary school, despite her mom always packing her a nutrition-approved bento box, and I think eating the candy neatly makes Tricia feel less guilty about having it. She's funny that way.

Stella politely finishes her turkey club, and I snap off another piece of my Twix. She grins like she's won the lottery when I hand it to her. At this rate, my mom's going to need to upgrade me to jumbo size.

The party committees meet with Mrs. Kalinack in the gym, where we'll have more space to spread out. Mrs. Kalinack has loaded up a cart with supplies we might need, like poster board and sequins and extra-big easel paper. Mr. Fallon's boyfriend picked him up for an appointment right after school this afternoon, so he has no idea. The bus kids even waited on the bus line so he wouldn't suspect anything, and then as soon as he was around the corner, Mrs. Kalinack gave them the all clear to duck out. We are coordinated like that at Pine Hill Elementary School.

Our babysitter, Altagracia, who usually only comes on Tuesdays, when my parents work late, is picking Manuel up from school today while I'm at this meeting.

Laurita walks over to me in the gym. "Want to go work over there?" she asks, pointing to an empty corner near the basketball hoop.

"Yeah, should we get some art supplies?" I eye the cart. There's some really good stuff there.

"We need to work on our research and write a first draft. Then we can transfer everything to poster board and tape the posters around the gym. The party guests can have their snacks while they walk around and read the posters."

I shrug and sit down cross-legged under the basketball hoop.

Laurita hunches over her notebook, and she reminds me a little bit of a turtle. Across the gym, Tricia is standing on a ladder motioning to Stella and Abdul. Lucas is holding the base. She's probably explaining where all the streamers will go. Jayden is sitting with Madan and Sarah, who has a recipe book spread across her lap. Everyone else looks like they're having fun.

Laurita points to the door that leads from the hallway to the gym. There's another door straight into the gym from outside. "Which door do you think should be the beginning of the exhibit?"

"If parents come, it'll be from outside, won't it?" This is so boring.

Laurita writes *Exhibit begins—back door* in her notebook. "I was thinking," she goes on, "that we could organize the exhibit in order of the history of immigration. Ellis Island in the 1890s, quota system in the 1920s, and family reunification today." She taps her pencil on her hand, thinking. "We should also talk about the border, and ICE."

"Huh?"

"Haven't you been paying attention during our immigration unit?"

I know I read some chapters in our social studies book and answered a few questions, but we haven't talked about it in class that much yet. It's only October.

Laurita sighs. "Well, you know about Ellis Island."

"Yeah, we visited last year." There was a joint field trip with all the fourth-grade classes in June. "It's the island where all the immigrants came, right near the Statue of Liberty."

"Exactly. So starting in the 1890s, immigrants from Europe came to Ellis Island. That could be our first poster board. Then, number two, in the 1920s—"

"So, like, a hundred years ago."

Laurita gives me a somewhat stern look and continues. "In the 1920s, the US made the quota system. They set up quotas, which are like caps, for immigrants from different countries, so only a certain number of people from each country could come."

"How did they decide how many people each country got?"

"It was two percent of however many people were in the United States from that country already, and no Asian countries were allowed."

"Wait a second," I say slowly. "There are a lot of countries. What if there weren't that many people from your country living in the United States but you really wanted to come? Like, if there wasn't a whole lot of food or apartments or medicine in your country?" Suddenly I remember some of the stories my parents have told me about what it was like living in Cuba when they were kids and teenagers, and I'm getting a prickly feeling inside.

"Then the US was all like, 'Stinks for you.' Basically everyone who got to come was from Europe."

I think about what Laurita's saying for a minute. It all sounds really unfair. *No one* from Asia was allowed to come? I look around the gym and imagine all the faces that wouldn't be here if that law still existed. I wonder if the quota system is like country clubs—like how they used to have rules excluding certain people but don't anymore. If it's one of those things that Laurita gets worked up about but that doesn't really bother anyone else.

"But that's not the law *anymore,* right?"

Laurita scribbles something else down in her notebook. "No. It changed in the 1960s. No more quotas."

"That's good!"

"Now immigration is supposed to be for family reunification. Like if you have a mom or a dad in another country, you can bring them to the United States. Sometimes you can come if your work helps you get a visa—like Mr. Fallon. And sometimes refugees can come, too."

"That sounds a lot better." I don't know why, but I feel like I'm begging Laurita to tell me something good. I know a lot about visas because you need them to come here from Cuba—a visa is like permission from a government to visit a country, and my parents are always worrying about people getting them. Yolanda and Álvaro got them because they're going to be in a fancy performance at the Met, but lots of other people we know can't.

I should know by now that Laurita didn't get the name Bad News Machine for nothing. She shrugs. "I mean, my family and your family got here, so that's good. But my grandmother is stuck in the Dominican Republic and she's probably going to die there."

She says it with the same tone someone else might say, "I don't want to empty the dishwasher but I guess I have to." Except she's not hunched over like a turtle anymore; she's sitting up with her fists clenched at her side. If she had long fingernails, they would leave marks.

I study Laurita carefully. Her skin is darker than mine, and her hair is curly like Regina's. But instead of a bun like Regina, Laurita puts hers in a ponytail. She has little tiny freckles across her nose. I'm used to seeing her with her mitt, walking home from school or throwing herself fly balls in her front yard. Without her softball gear, she looks smaller and not nearly as tough.

"I'm—I'm really sorry," I say.

Laurita just shrugs again.

"Isn't—didn't you say that now there's no quota? So if it's family reunification—"

Laurita hunches over her notebook again. "Yeah, but now there's a long line even to get them to read your application. They're never going to get around to my abuela." She traces one of the spiral rings in her notebook with her pencil, pressing hard to make dark gray marks. "Plus, it's different now. They've made it so hard to immigrate that a lot of Latino people have to cross the border on foot. They have to hike through the desert and worry about ICE—Immigration and Customs Enforcement."

"Laurita," I say, "your abuela lives in *the Dominican Republic*. That's an island. There's no way she's coming here on foot."

"Yeah, and she's old," Laurita says. "But a lot of people from the islands do cross the border, Sofía. They fly to a country where you can get to the United States on foot because it's a better shot than waiting around forever for a visa."

I've seen the news, and what Laurita is saying sounds terrifying. "Yikes," I say. "I really hope your abuela can get here. It's—it's not fair, what happens at the border."

"Nope," Laurita says. "It's not. But you know what? It doesn't even bother most people in Pine Hill. They just think Latino immigrants are criminals."

"That's not true," I protest. "People in Pine Hill are nice." What is Laurita talking about? All of my friends live in Pine Hill. *We* live in Pine Hill. I definitely don't think Latino immigrants are criminals.

I'm about to open my mouth to say something, but then

I remember what happened to Yolanda when she was buying coffee this morning. How one of our neighbors got mad just because Yolanda has an accent. I close my mouth without saying anything.

Laurita gestures around the gym at everyone talking and having fun with their committees. "Can you imagine Pine Hill Elementary School having a party like this for someone in *our* families?"

CHAPTER TWELVE

It's hard to stop thinking about what Laurita said. It's like she planted a seed in my mind and I'm trying not to water it, but the seed keeps growing and growing.

On Friday evening, I help my mom load up the rice into the cooker while she stirs the beans. Yolanda and Álvaro are in the city for a rehearsal, and Manuel and Regina have approximately six thousand friends over. Eva and Jonah are outside with Manuel making giant leaf piles and then jumping in them, and Regina and her friends Bridgit and Cassadie are up in our room. They kicked me out, even though I was minding my own business, sitting on my bed and browsing through a book of ballet costumes I got from the library. Okay, I was listening in, but only a little. Only to the parts where Regina was telling Bridgit and Cassadie how she's nervous about being Dewdrop because this is her big shot—if she nails this role and her audition tapes are amazing, she could be invited to the Summer Intensive at ABT. That part wasn't very interesting, because everyone *knows* Regina is going to be the best Dew-drop in history. But what I *didn't* know is that if she does really well at the Summer Intensive, she could be invited to join the ABT Studio Company (which is kind of like a farm team). It would mean she would have to move to New York City and finish school online instead of at Pine Hill High School. That's the part when I stopped reading my book and started paying attention, because I had no idea Regina was planning on leaving us all so soon. Bridgit and Cassadie were hanging on her every word and too busy to notice me, but Regina saw me listening in and kicked me out of the room before I could ask any questions.

I don't mind hanging out with my mom, though. Every once in a while Davy zooms through the kitchen, running back and forth between Manuel and his friends outside and Regina and her friends upstairs. It's a little bit unfair, but Regina's friends think Davy is like their personal toy doll and they let him hang out with them as long as he wants. He cuddles up next to Regina and plays with her collection of Treasure Trolls, which she still has lined up on the shelf above her bed, even though, you guessed it, she never touches them. If you're wondering why the Treasure Trolls get to stay when my stuffies all get the church treatment, it's because Treasure Trolls are collectors' items. Apparently some people buy them for a lot of money. Also, my mom claims that my stuffies get grody and their fur falls out, whereas Regina's Treasure Trolls are in mint condition. There's a lot of injustice in the Acosta family where old toys are concerned.

"Mami," I say after setting the timer on the rice cooker, "when you became a United States citizen, did you have a party?"

"Ay, sí," my mom replies. "Tu tía Rosi y tu tía Aldema me hicieron la gran fiesta en Miami."

I've actually heard about this party before. It was before I was born, but my mom likes to talk about how Aldema flew up from Puerto Rico and they celebrated at Rosi's house in Miami. My cousin Roberto was a little baby. My mom always says that any occasion where all three sisters are together is a special one, and there's a picture of them in nice dresses, with Roberto in Rosi's arms. It's sitting on the mantel next to the picture of Yolanda right now.

"Not a family party," I insist, "a *work* party. Like at your school."

My mom wrinkles her nose. "A *work* party? Why would they throw me a party at work?"

"I don't know, because they liked you?"

"Me pagan, eso es suficiente," my mom replies with a laugh. "As long as the school pays my salary, I'm not too worried about parties."

My mom rustles around the refrigerator, and I practice some *frappés* at the kitchen counter, imagining my foot is a match that I'm trying to strike on the floor. Mrs. Jansen told us to think of that during our last class, and I like pretending that my leg can light a fire.

"So did you and Papi have to stop at Ellis Island when you came here?"

"At *Ellis Island?*" My mom straightens up and closes the refrigerator door. "Sofía Carmen, how old do you think I am?"

I stop mid-*frappé*. "I dunno. Old?"

My mom starts laughing like a hyena.

"So if you didn't come through Ellis Island—then you came with the quota system!" I add triumphantly, remembering what Laurita taught me. But now my mom is all out howling with laughter.

"¿Qué pasó?" my dad asks, coming in from the living room.

"Your daughter"—my mom clutches her side—"thinks you and I came to this country through Ellis Island. On a boat. Or maybe through the quota system."

My dad laughs his short, booming laughs, his hand on his stomach.

I roll my eyes. I try to remember what Laurita said. I know the order was Ellis Island, quota, then family reunification. I had just forgotten that Ellis Island and the quota system were a really long time ago. Laurita also said most of the immigrants who came then were from Europe, so I guess it would have been sort of surprising for my parents to come from Cuba that way.

"Corazón, Ellis Island was closed a very long time ago, and there hasn't been a quota since the 1960s," my dad says, putting his arm around my shoulder.

I try to sound smart and mature, the way Regina does when she talks to my parents. You would think they'd be more impressed by all I learned from Laurita today, but it's like you mix up one little detail and suddenly you're a comedy act. "So if you didn't come during the quota system, did you come for family reunification?"

My mom stops laughing, and I see her eyes meet my dad's. "We were different, Sofía. We're Cuban, and we're ballet dancers."

"So?"

My mom drops gracefully into a chair. It's weird to see her *sitting* in the kitchen; she's always cooking or cleaning when she's in here. "You remember how your papi and I met when we were in the Ballet Nacional de Cuba?"

It's not like I could forget, with the two of them constantly telling stories about it.

"One year, the ballet company went on a performance tour in Germany."

I know this part of the story already. The director of a German ballet company saw my parents dance and asked them if they wanted to stay in Germany and become soloists at his company. They danced there for a while and then moved to New York City.

"Era difícil, deciding whether to stay in Germany," my mom says. "It meant leaving behind our families and everything—everyone, really—that we knew."

My dad stands behind my mom, rubbing her shoulders. "Pero ya tú sabes, Sofía. Things were difficult in Cuba then. We lived with my mom in a tiny place and we didn't know whether we would ever be able to find our own apartment. We couldn't imagine buying a car or a house or having a pantry packed with food." My dad waves at our pantry closet, which is currently stuffed with the entire neighborhood's favorite treats. It had never occurred to me before, but maybe this is why my mom always buys so many munchies, while every other mom in our neighborhood is telling their kids to stop eating so many processed snacks—maybe my mom never really had the *option* of having a pantry full of Choco Chunks and Chewy Bars before, and she's not going to let it slip through her fingers now.

"Pero lo *peor*," my mom says, holding a finger in the air, "was breaking the news to Alicia."

"Alicia Alonso?" I whisper her name.

My mom nods her head. "The year we left for Germany, Alicia was still alive and well, directing the Ballet Nacional de Cuba. She was furious that we abandoned Cuba. That was the last conversation I ever had with her. It broke my heart."

I think about how my mom and Regina both have the middle name Alicia, after Cuba's great *prima ballerina as-*

soluta. I think about how Regina tries to dance just like Alicia did, feeling the music through her feet, and how excited my parents are that ABT is doing a tribute to Alicia this spring. I can't imagine my mom doing anything to make Alicia mad.

Suddenly I have a thought. "But, Mami, *Alicia* didn't always live in Cuba! She danced with ABT, remember? That's why Regina wants to be in ABT someday—and Manuel and me, too," I add quickly.

"Alicia practically *founded* ABT," my dad says proudly. "She was one of the people who helped bring classical ballet to the United States and establish a world-class ballet company here. ABT and Alicia—son lo mismo. Están unidos."

Davy bursts through the door of the kitchen. "I jumped so high!" He leaps into my mom's lap. "I was higher than Jonah—than Jonah climbing a big rock!"

My mom pats Davy on the back and glances out the kitchen window at Manuel and Eva and Jonah building a leaf pile that's going to be taller than Jonah standing on a rock soon, too. "Sofía, ve y díles que ya es hora de entrar. It's getting dark."

I stop with my hand on the door and turn back. "Hey, Ma," I say. "When you came to the United States from Germany, *then* did you use family reunification?"

My mom shakes her head. "We got visas to the United States because we were invited as guests of a ballet company in North Carolina. Like I said, it's different for dancers."

My dad walks over to the door with me. I could use some backup wrangling Manuel and his crew. "Además," he says, "twenty years ago, when your mami and I first came to this country, basically any Cuban who made it to the US could apply for citizenship."

"So you—got all those rights and responsibilities?"

"That's one way of putting it," my dad says. "To me, becoming a citizen means being protected by the government. I'm not saying we've had it easy, but at least we knew we would always have a home here, and no one could threaten us like they do other immigrants."

I had thought a heart would be a good decoration for the citizenship poster in the gym exhibit, but now I don't know if it's such a good idea anymore. If being a citizen is like being in a family, what kind of family is so mean about who's in and who's out? I wish the United States could be a family like Davy says the Acostas are, an accordion that just gets bigger.

"We're lucky we could become citizens just by showing up," my mom explains.

"And that was *only* Cubans? Everyone else had to become a citizen the other ways?"

"Solo los cubanos," my mom says. "It was part of how the United States tried to fight communism. By getting Cubans to leave the island. It wasn't fair, but it did make it easier for us to become United States citizens."

"Wow, Cubans are lucky," I say quietly.

My dad claps his hands from the porch, signaling for Manuel and his friends to come inside. "¡Ya deben tener hambre!" He ushers them into the kitchen and rattles off all the food my mom has just made, then turns back to me. "As I like to say, qué rico ser cubano. It's good to be Cuban."

I tail my dad through the kitchen and into the living room. "But what about *now*? Could a Cuban still become a citizen just by showing up?"

My dad isn't smiling anymore. In fact, his face suddenly seems so wrinkled and pale it's as if he just went through a costume quick-change. He doesn't meet my eyes. "No, mi cielo. Now Cubans have to cross the border, like other Latino immigrants have been doing for a long time. Ahora nada es fácil. Not for Latinos, at least."

My dad doesn't say it, but there's something in his tone that reminds me of what Laurita said at school. As rico as it is to be Cuban, my black beans and rice barely taste like anything that night.

CHAPTER THIRTEEN

Tricia is coming to my house on a weekday! This *never* happens, but Tricia's mom is busy Tuesday when there's a half day at school, so Tricia's going to walk home with Manuel and me and spend the rest of the day with us and Altagracia.

"Good," Regina says when she hears the news. "Tricia can help you learn the Grandfather Dance. You're still mixing up the steps."

I ignore Regina and bounce on my bed, chanting, "Tricia is coming! Tricia is coming!"

The very next chance I get, I race down to the basement and go to my spot behind the boiler. I get to work on our cardboard theater so I can show Tricia how great it's looking. While I work, I hold Jingle, Solarie, and Mr. Rumpkins in my lap and think about what I could use as the Christmas tree for the cardboard stage. The three stuffed animals could be the audience when it's done. And my mom says I don't use them anymore!

* * *

Mr. Fallon is a great teacher, but even he can't make the school day speed up. At journal time I ignore the prompt and just write *Tricia is coming!* in my notebook and write about how excited I am to show her our miniature stage.

At dismissal I link arms with Tricia and race out the door. Stella follows right behind us, and Tricia loops back to link her other arm with Stella, dragging me with her. The three of us make a chain and weave across the lawn toward the second/third-grade door, crashing into Lucas and Abdul, who are waiting on the bus line, as we run.

"Hey!" Abdul yells. "That's the *second* time you crashed into me, Sofía Acosta!"

I wave my free hand in a try-and-catch-me gesture and skip the rest of the way to the door, Tricia and Stella giggling beside me.

"Manuel!" I call, seeing the top of his head in the crowd of kids.

He waves back at me, and his hair bounces up and down as he runs down the stairs.

Ms. Linski, Manuel's teacher, is right behind him. She holds open the door and smiles at him. She has the whitest, straightest teeth you've ever seen. It's like she came right out of a dentist commercial. "Adiós, Emmanuel," she says.

"Bye, Emmanuel!" yells a kid I've never seen before.

"Hold on a second," I say, shaking my arm free from the

Tricia-and-Stella chain. I stop Manuel on the edge of the school lawn. "Manuel, why did that kid call you Emmanuel? And why was Ms. Linski speaking in Spanish?" She said *adiós* like some kind of cartoon character, separating the *i* and the *o* sounds instead of making a *yo* sound like you're supposed to when you see an *i* and an *o* together in Spanish.

Manuel shrugged. "That's just what Ms. Linski calls me. She likes saying things in Spanish."

"Does she *speak* Spanish?" Other kids push past, and Tricia and Stella just stand there. Stella's mouth is hanging open, and Tricia is looking up at the sky like she can't hear anything we're saying.

"She can say *hola*. And *perfect-o*." Manuel thinks for a minute. "Oh, and she says *no entiendo* sometimes. Like if I make a mistake in math class."

"But you speak English!" I burst out. "She can't not understand you! And *perfect-o* is barely a word." I look at Tricia for confirmation that this is the most outrageous thing I've ever heard, but she's still pretending to be fascinated by a cumulus cloud. This weekday playdate isn't turning out the way I expected.

"You have to tell her to stop it. Also, Manuel *is* your name in Spanish! Why would she change it to Emmanuel?" I throw my hands in the air.

Manuel doesn't seem too fussed. "Everyone thinks it's really funny."

"I'm telling Mami and Papi they have to talk to her. Or write you a note."

"No!!!" Manuel's left mitten slips off, and he snatches it up from the sidewalk. He flaps his arms at his side and pleads, "If Mami and Papi talk to her and she makes everyone stop calling me Emmanuel, they'll just laugh at me. Plus, she'll hate me and I'll get bad grades."

I want to tell Manuel that if you're eight years old and the only grades you can get are a 1, 2, 3, or 4, it's not that big a deal, but his eyes are so big and round and begging that I just look down at him quietly, trying to decide what to do.

Tricia seems to have remembered she's a part of this group. "Give Ms. Linski a break, Sofía," Tricia says. "You've never even met her, and if Manuel thinks it's funny, then that's what matters, right?"

Manuel's shoulders drop in relief.

"But it's—mean. It's not right."

My eyes meet Stella's, and she bites her lip.

"You're right," Stella says. "It's not nice of Ms. Linski to make up a name without asking permission."

"It's awful!" I burst out.

"But," Stella goes on, and for some reason all three of us are looking at her like she's the grown-up here, "she probably wasn't trying to be mean. Everyone says she's one of the nicest teachers."

Just then Stella's mom pulls up and honks the horn. She

rolls down the window and offers us all a ride, but we live so close to the school there's no point.

"Gotta go!" Stella hops into the car. "Don't worry about it, Sofía," she says as she slams the door, like she's trying to comfort me, except I don't feel any better.

The whole walk home, while Manuel drags his wheelie backpack, I fume to Tricia about how unbelievable Ms. Linski is being.

"Will you take a breath?" Tricia complains as we're turning onto our sidewalk. "She didn't mean anything and now you're making a big deal out of it. Lately you're like Laurita, always whining about something."

I close my mouth tight. I am *not* like Laurita. I'm not a Bad News Machine, and I'm not super serious all the time. To prove it, I switch to telling Tricia about the cardboard theater, and she gets excited to work on it too. She wants to look at my craft supplies so we can talk about the headpieces for the Decorations Committee, which sort of annoys me, but I figure I've already done all the complaining I can get away with today.

At home, Altagracia is breading chicken cutlets for dinner that night.

"¡Hola, niños!" she says as we troop in the door. "¿Qué tal la escuela? ¡Milagro que Manuel no trajo a los gemelos!"

Manuel explains that Eva and Jonah had dentist appointments, which is why he doesn't have a playdate for the first time in the history of his life, and shoots off to the couch to play video games. Just then the front door opens again, and Yolanda and Álvaro walk into the kitchen. Álvaro's carrying a ballet bag on his shoulder and wearing an enormous puffy coat from my dad. It looks silly to have on such a big coat so early in the fall, but I guess if you come from Cuba, it seems really cold out. Yolanda and Álvaro give Altagracia kisses and she takes Álvaro's ballet bag like they've all known each other a thousand years.

"How was the Met?" I ask, and Yolanda and Álvaro tell me they just got a special tour from the artistic director of ABT, who is organizing the joint performance.

"That is SO COOL!" I shriek, and I'm about to ask them a million questions about what it's like and whether it's true that there's a whole floor just for making wigs and another whole floor just for making shoes when Altagracia clears her throat, and I remember that I haven't introduced Tricia. Introducing new people is a pretty strict rule at my house.

"Esta es mi amiga Tricia," I tell everyone, putting my hand on Tricia's shoulder proudly.

Altagracia grins. "¡La famosa Tricia!"

Yolanda claps her hands together and says in Spanish that as soon as she's had a shower, we'll all have a snack and get to know each other, and Álvaro holds out his hand to shake.

I'm beaming like a flashlight. It's like I just brought home a celebrity.

After all the exclaiming and clapping and smiling has quieted down, Altagracia asks Tricia how she is.

Tricia looks at me nervously. "Um, could you tell them I don't speak Spanish?"

I pause. "They know that already. They were just saying hello."

Tricia gives a short, quick wave, like she's afraid something might bite off her hand. Suddenly everyone gets very busy. Yolanda and Álvaro say they need to put down their things upstairs, and I grab some Chewy Bars from the cabinet and pull Tricia toward the basement. I think it probably would have been easier if Tricia had just said hello to everyone in English instead of making such a big deal about not speaking Spanish. Actually, come to think of it, right then would have been a good time for some Ms. Linski–level *hola* and *adiós* skills. But all I want to do is change the subject, fast-forward past who speaks Spanish and who doesn't, and get to the part where my best friend and I are doing crafts and laughing together. I run down the last five steps of the basement stairs.

CHAPTER FOURTEEN

After Tricia's mom comes to pick her up, I sit in the basement and work on a miniature Party Scene dress I've been
sewing for a Barbie doll. I pretend I'm working on one of
the *real* Party Scene dresses, adding bows and lace to the
fringe. I think about Tricia. Mrs. Rivera is white, but Tricia's
dad's parents were Cuban. They must have spoken Spanish,
but they died before Tricia was born. I wonder if Tricia would
feel different talking to my family if she'd known her grandparents. Maybe she would know how to say hi to people who
speak Spanish without being rude. Maybe she would know
what it's like to have family visit from a long way away. Or
maybe it would have been exactly the same. Maybe Tricia just
sees things differently than I do. I'm still sewing and thinking
through it when Yolanda's voice pierces the quiet of my hiding place.

I stiffen. Yolanda is about halfway down the stairs, talking
to Álvaro in low, urgent tones.

I try to tune them out, but their words are like *frappés,* sharp and striking.

"No puedes," Yolanda pleads. "You could be caught."

Álvaro laughs a short, hollow laugh. "Mamá, it's not like that anymore. You *know* it isn't," he says resentfully.

"¡Mira a Eduardo!"

"What about him?" Álvaro retorts. "He's doing great. He has a good job. He's dancing *lead* roles. And new repertoire. ¡Imagínate!"

"Sí, pero is the company doing anything to help him? Is he ever going to become a citizen? I don't want you living in the shadows, Álvaro, tú no sabes—"

"And I don't want to live under my mother's thumb forever!"

"Eso no es justo," Yolanda says, all hurt and resentment. "Yo *nunca*—I never tried to control you."

There's silence for a minute, and I try very hard not to breathe or rustle fabric. I want to stretch my leg, which is suddenly cramped, but I stay frozen in place.

Yolanda switches gears. "Los Latinos en este país—the *racism,* Álvaro. Haven't you watched the news? They talk about Latinos like we're criminals, they call us bad guys—that's the United States. Why would you want to live here?"

I swallow hard, remembering what that lady said to Yolanda at the checkout counter.

"The Acostas seem to have it pretty good."

"Ay, Álvaro, no seas majadero," Yolanda replies impatiently. "Los Acostas son gente de mucho privilegio. Siempre lo han sido. When we were kids in Havana, Carmen always had it good."

A knot twists in the pit of my stomach. Yolanda is telling Álvaro that it's different for us, that we're kind of fancy. She doesn't say it in a mean tone, but it holds bitterness all the same. A part of me wants to shout up that if we had so many privileges, no one at school would call my brother Emmanuel and make jokes about him speaking Spanish or dancing ballet. I want to tell them that the fancy people are the ones who are members of the country club and live in Pine Hill Heights and don't have weekday playdates, not us. I want it to be true that Álvaro could move here and have a house in Pine Hill anytime. But then I think about my dad's face when he told me that Cubans today don't have it as easy as they used to. I think about Álvaro's dark skin. I think about Laurita asking me if Pine Hill Elementary would ever have a party for someone in one of our families. I keep my mouth shut.

"I'm going to think it over," Álvaro says. "Just—give me some time, okay?"

Yolanda sighs loudly, and I hear the stairs creak as she leaves.

I don't know how long I sit there. At some point I hear Álvaro's weight settling down on the stairs above me. The house is very, very quiet. There are no creaking floorboards, as if the bricks and beams are holding their breath.

After a long time, I crawl out from my hiding spot. I bring

Solarie with me, just to have some company. Then I climb up to sit next to Álvaro near the top of the stairs. He's surprised to see me.

"¿Nos oíste?"

"I heard the whole thing." I squirm.

Álvaro nods, staring straight ahead. "I've been offered a contract. As a soloist."

"With ABT?" My jaw drops. Álvaro is only seventeen years old. Being a soloist with the greatest ballet company in the world—if I thought Regina was good, Álvaro must be *really* good.

"Yep. The artistic director saw me practicing today. He told me on the spot he could give me a job."

"So—you're going to take it, right? ABT is like—well, it can't get any better than that, can it?"

Álvaro glances over at me. "Your sister sure brainwashed you, huh?"

"No," I retort defensively. "I've seen ABT perform lots of times. They're the *best.*"

"But you've never seen the Ballet Nacional de Cuba."

"I love the Ballet Nacional de Cuba!" He's right that I've never actually seen them dance before, but I will when Álvaro is in his performance, and I've heard so many stories about the company from my parents. "I love ABT *and* the Ballet Nacional de Cuba *both,*" I say passionately. "Just like Alicia Alonso loved them *both* and helped start *both* of them."

Álvaro laughs. "Even more like your sister."

I shrug. "Sometimes Regina is right about things." I want to make Álvaro laugh for real, so I add, "Not about dancing with your eyes closed or practicing until all hours of the night on weekends, but about *some* stuff—"

I'm so happy when Álvaro laughs again. "It would be hard to leave home," he muses. "Especially if my mom won't follow me. I'll miss my friends. I like my life in Cuba."

It's an impossible choice. Passing up becoming a soloist in ABT would be—well, who would give up a chance like that? But then I imagine being away from my mom and my friends, maybe forever, and a cold shiver runs up my spine. I would never be brave enough.

"You know what they used to call it when dancers left Cuba for other countries?"

"What?" I ask.

"Defecting."

"That makes it sound like you're defective!" I blurt out.

Álvaro nods. "Sí, señorita. People will say nasty things about me—like I betrayed my country."

Heat rushes to my face. "But *I* won't think you're defective. My parents won't either. And none of the people who come see you dance at ABT will think you're defective. They'll just think you're the best ballet dancer in the world. They'll shower you with flowers. We'll yell '*Bravo!!!*'" I clap my hands to the side and make a face like I'm a very snooty lady at the

Metropolitan Opera House, cheering for the brilliant young soloist from Cuba, Álvaro Ruiz. I get another laugh out of him.

Álvaro shakes his head and jabs me with his elbow jokingly. "You're going to give me an ego."

"I'm good at that," I say with a very straight face. "Have you met my brother and sister?"

More laughter. This is getting to be a regular comedy act.

"When I'm dancing with ABT," Álvaro says slowly, and it sounds like he's already made up his mind, "I'll be lucky to have you as my almost–little sister."

Now it's my turn to laugh. "More like you'll have Regina as your almost–little sister. I'm never going to make it anywhere near a professional ballet company. Have you seen me clap a rhythm?"

Álvaro smirks. "It's pretty bad."

"Hey!"

"You said so yourself!" He throws up his hands. "Pero, hermanita, you know that family isn't just who gets into which ballet company. Not all of the Acostas have to be ballet dancers."

I shake my head. "Are you kidding me?" I'm going to sound like Laurita, but it's true. "You think they let Latinos who *aren't* famous dancers live in Pine Hill? Look around." I gesture as if we're looking down at the town from a hill instead of on the basement steps.

Álvaro shrugs. "At least you have your family. The Acostas have a welcoming home with a lot of amor y alegría."

"That's true. Our neighbor Davy calls it the Acosta Accordion. Because sometimes it's big"—I mime stretching an accordion wide—"and sometimes it's small." I squish the imaginary accordion closed.

"That's the little guy always at the fence, right?"

"Yep."

"Cute." Álvaro stands up, stretching his back as he does. "You know it's a secret, right?"

"Defecting?"

"If anyone found out, I could be in big trouble."

I gulp.

"I'm serious, Sofía. You can't even tell your parents or Regina. *Especially* not them. They know too many people in the ballet world. They could let it slip."

I draw a zip across my lips and throw away the imaginary key. Álvaro nods sharply and turns up the stairs.

CHAPTER FIFTEEN

It's time to get *going*. That's what Mrs. Jansen tells us in rehearsal at the beginning of November, and that's what I tell Mrs. Lewis in the costume closet. I'm helping her sort through the costumes and make a list of what repairs need to be done, so I'm here with permission for a change. I point out the missing beads on the Dewdrop costume, and Mrs. Lewis taps her clipboard with her pen.

"You know what, Sofía? How would you like to do the beads for that costume?"

"By myself? But I'm a kid."

Mrs. Lewis laughs. "When I was your age, I was already on a serger. I think you can handle some beading."

I am very impressed. Sergers are expensive sewing machines like the kind that make clothing for stores. I've never touched one.

"I would *love* to do the beads for Regina's Dewdrop costume," I say quickly. "And while I'm at it, could I do the trim for the Party Scene dresses?" I pull one of the dresses out on its hanger and show Mrs. Lewis how the lace is wearing off. "I have a lot of ideas. I was thinking we could add lace and ribbon and maybe little tiny rosettes."

"Absolutely!"

"I'll ask my mom when we can go buy the trims, and then I'll come here and help, like, every rehearsal break I get," I promise.

"No, baby girl," Mrs. Lewis replies, and I grin because I love it when she calls me that—like I'm family and not just another kid from ballet. "Let's save your poor mother a trip. The next time I go to the shop, I'll pick you up and we'll get everything we need."

When it's time to go back to my rehearsal, all I can think of is how gorgeous everyone will look dressed up for Party Scene. Greg has to pull me around even more than usual during the Grandfather Dance.

After we're done, Mrs. Jansen gives us corrections before we try it again.

"Tricia," I whisper while Mrs. Jansen is showing proper foot positions, "I'm going to go shopping with Mrs. Lewis and—"

"Shhh!" Tricia hisses back at me. "I really want to get this right." She angles her head to the side and mimics Mrs. Jansen's feet.

Sheesh, everyone is acting like *The Nutcracker* is tomorrow instead of weeks away. I close my eyes and imagine all the beautiful trimmings I'm going to get for our costumes, until Greg nudges me that it's time to run through the dance again.

When everyone else is packing up, Mrs. Jansen asks me to stay behind.

"Sofía," she says once the studio has cleared out. "Do you even *want* to be in Party Scene?"

Is she kidding me? I've been wanting to be in Party Scene since Regina was in it three years ago. Of course I do. It's basically the best part a fifth grader can have.

Mrs. Jansen sighs. "This is a serious performance, Sofía. This isn't just *The Nutcracker* danced by the children at a local neighborhood dance school. This is a preprofessional production."

"But this *is* my local neighborhood dance school," I blurt out. All the kids in the show are from Pine Hill or East Bolton—that's, like, two towns that aren't even very big.

Wrong thing to say. Mrs. Jansen stomps her black boot for my attention. "What I *mean*, Sofía, is that this isn't a production for people who are goofing off. This is a show for serious aspiring ballet dancers. Do you really want to jeopardize Regina's chances of getting into American Ballet Theatre?"

"What does my Party Scene have to do with Regina?"

"The dance community doesn't only judge the individual dancer, Sofía; they judge how professional the performance is as a whole."

I stare at the floor. "I don't want to mess things up for Regina," I say. "It's just that Party Scene is hard."

Mrs. Jansen leads me toward my position in the Grandfather Dance. "I only have a few minutes before Regina gets here for her rehearsal. But let's go over that hop-step. You can't keep bumping into other people every time you jump backward."

"Okay. I can try." But I don't have much hope.

We hop-step until I'm like the world's tiredest bunny rabbit. Mrs. Jansen plays the same four bars of music over and over again, but I don't see how anyone is supposed to do this step on time. You have to hop up, *backward,* and have your feet land exactly together in a neat *plié.* How are you supposed to see where your feet are landing if you're going backward? And no, you're not allowed to look down. You have to look up at your partner and smile like you're at a party. Plus, there's more of this upbeat-downbeat stuff. You have to *land* on the downbeat and *hop* on the upbeat, but I have no idea how I'm supposed to control when my feet land from a jump, even if I could hear the difference between upbeats and downbeats and weren't pretty sure everyone is making them up.

I tell Mrs. Jansen this, and she covers her eyes with her hand. "Sofía, they're your feet. *Tell* them when to land."

"But they're in the air!"

"From the top," Mrs. Jansen says wearily.

By the time Regina arrives, Mrs. Jansen and I are both

pretty frustrated. Regina leans casually in the doorway, watching me hop up and down, and I feel like I'm under a laser beam.

"I'll help her at home," Regina says to Mrs. Jansen, heading to the barre to get herself warmed up.

I *hate* it when Regina says she'll help me with ballet. It's like she's rubbing it in that she's the perfect Acosta ballerina and I'm the mess-up little sister.

"Sofía," Mrs. Jansen says seriously. "You need to practice *every day*. Otherwise we're going to have to find someone else to take your spot. Do you understand? Every. Day."

"Okay, okay!" I promise. "I'll be hopping in my sleep." I put my hands up by my chin and bounce out of the room like a bunny, but neither Regina nor Mrs. Jansen so much as smiles.

The waiting area and dressing room are completely empty. Everyone left already, including Mrs. Lewis. Tricia and Stella are gone, because they don't need extra help with ballet, and my older sister is in the studio, being a star. Only Manuel is waiting for me.

"Mami and Papi are in the car," he announces. "I told them I would wait here for you."

I grip Manuel's warm hand tightly as we head to my parents' car, grateful to have at least one Acosta I can hang on to.

CHAPTER SIXTEEN

Of course my parents find out why Mrs. Jansen kept me late, and of course my mom's reaction is all "Challenge accepted!" So now my house is like rehearsal city. Luckily, I have lots of sewing projects to distract me. This Saturday Yolanda is taking me into the city for fabric shopping, and Sunday Mrs. Lewis is taking me to a fabric store in East Bolton to get trimmings for the Party Scene dresses. It's like a double whammy of costume beautifulness.

Shopping with Yolanda is awesome. My mom packs us snacks, and we ride the train into New York City munching all the way. At the beginning it's a little awkward, but I don't have to talk to Yolanda that much, because we're so busy eating. By the time the train rolls into Grand Central Terminal, I've already forgotten that I'm still getting to know Yolanda and that it was ever weird being alone with her. Instead, we chat about fabric and costumes as we walk off the train and into the station, where the ceiling is painted with patterns of stars, then out into the frantic city. I stay close to Yolanda on the sidewalk, holding her hand so that the crowds of people don't push us apart. Once we're a few blocks away from the station, it gets a little less packed and we can talk more easily. Yolanda is telling me all sorts of interesting stories about costumes for shows she has been in. One time, she was traveling with the Ballet Nacional de Cuba and they changed her part at the last minute—but hadn't brought the right costume for the change. Yolanda made what she needed out of curtains from the hotel window!

Even though she lives all the way in Havana and has only been to New York once before, Yolanda expertly navigates the city, and she knows the best fabric stores. They're all in the same neighborhood, little shops piled with bolts of fabric up to the ceiling, crammed in next to one another on the same block. We go into shop after shop, and Yolanda picks out black fabric with gold braiding for the trim. Álvaro is going to look striking in it.

I search each store carefully, looking for what I want to buy. In one store, I spot a gauzy fabric, just a little bit more purple than periwinkle. I ask the store clerk to get it down for me, and Yolanda and I roll it out on the cutting table.

"I bet I could make Regina a skirt from this," I say. As the storekeeper is cutting the fabric and bundling it up, I spot a bolt of cotton with a pattern of characters from Manuel's favorite video game. I point to it and ask for a quarter yard. I'm going to make Manuel a new headband.

When we're leaving the store, Yolanda asks me if I want to get anything for myself.

"I already did."

"I meant to make something for you, not for your siblings."

I shake my head. "Dance skirts look better on Regina. It's because she's so good at ballet. Besides, I want to do something for Manuel." I can't tell Yolanda about how I think Manuel's friends might be bullying him, or about how his teacher calls him Emmanuel, but I do want to make him something special.

"What about headbands for your friends?" Yolanda says with a smile. "We could make something for—cómo se llama—Tricia!"

I laugh. "I'm already making her and another girl matching headpieces for school."

Yolanda wrinkles her brow. "And one for yourself?"

I explain how Tricia and Stella are on a different committee from me and there's no way Laurita is going to wear matching headpieces, so no.

I can tell from Yolanda's face that she doesn't think this makes any sense. "I see. This is the girl who didn't know how to say hello."

"Tricia's nice," I say. "She's been my best friend since we were little. It's just—" I try to think of what to say. I don't know how to explain to Yolanda that even though Tricia doesn't want to have matching headpieces with me and gets nervous around people in my family who speak Spanish, she's still the only person I can talk to about my secret stuffed-animal stash. She's the only other kid who does crafts with me. "She's my friend," I say finally.

Yolanda nods wisely. "All friends have tension sometimes. Tu mamá y yo—" She shakes her head, laughing.

"Wait, you used to fight with my *mom*?" I ask incredulously. "My mom talks about you like you're a saint!"

Yolanda bursts out laughing and takes my hand to head back to the train station. "Oh, sí," she says, "we've had some big fights in our day. You know, when I separated from Álvaro's dad, your mom wanted me to move to the United States."

"Why didn't you? That would have been cool!"

"Because," Yolanda says simply, "Cuba is my home. I have a job at the Ballet Nacional de Cuba. I have family there. I couldn't just pick up and leave."

Right. In my family, almost everyone has left Cuba. My mom's sisters both live in the United States now. But if Yolanda left Cuba, she would be leaving so many people behind. I get a wriggly feeling in my stomach, thinking about how Yolanda will feel if Álvaro moves to the United States. And even though Álvaro said he would think it over, he sounded pretty sure when I talked to him on the stairs.

"I thought about what your mom was saying," Yolanda goes on. "I really did. I wanted what was best for Álvaro, of course. But then I thought of how it felt for me when your mom left Cuba, and when so many of my other friends and relatives left. How much I hated being left behind. I couldn't do that to my community at home."

"So you told my mom you couldn't come? Then what happened?"

"Well," Yolanda says, "your mom didn't like that at all. You know how she is—she thinks she's right about everything."

I giggle. My mom *does* think she's right about everything. "So that's when you had a fight?"

Yolanda nods. "I thought she was never going to speak to me again! But she got over it. We both did. That's the way it is with real friends."

It's like when Regina and I fight—we don't really need to make up afterward, because our fights kind of evaporate. We forget about them when there's so much else going on. And even though Yolanda isn't actually our family, I get what she means. I don't really blame Tricia for anything. She doesn't know better. We may just be like Yolanda and my mom—sometimes we hit a rough patch, but we get over it. Because best friends are like almost-family. I slip my hand into Yolanda's again, and we walk confidently back toward Grand Central Terminal, and home.

CHAPTER SEVENTEEN

It looks like someone spilled a treasure chest onto my bed, except instead of jewels and gold coins, there are rhinestones, glistening beads, strips of velvet and lace, and tiny cloth flower buds. Last Sunday Mrs. Lewis took me to get everything I would need for the Party Scene costumes and Regina's Dewdrop costume. Afterward, she helped me carry the Party Scene dresses into our bedroom, and Regina had to move some of her stuff out of the way for a change. Mrs. Lewis stayed and talked to my mom the whole afternoon. I've been sewing ever since then.

It's two weeks before Thanksgiving and I've spread everything out on my bed so I can really get to work. It's nice to be sewing here and not the basement. Usually the sewing I do in my room is practical, like fixing Regina's pointe shoes. But anything really fun I hide—it's always stuff that I was supposed to donate to church! Now I hold strips of lace and velvet up to one of the Party Scene dresses. I pace around and look at the different trimmings from every angle, then grab the velvet. Sitting on the floor, I make tiny whipstitches, sewing the velvet strip to the bottom of the dress. I'm so focused on those little stitches that I barely even hear Regina on the phone, inviting her friends over.

The dress looks better, less ratty and more tied together, as soon as I finish sewing on the velvet. I beam at it and reach for a satin rosette. A lot of people would hot-glue these on, but that looks drippy sometimes, and anyway my parents don't love me using hot glue. So I poke the needle through the center of the rosette and attach it with tight stitches. I love how the rosette is smooth, with just a little bit of shine. I grab three more in the same color. I can't wait to show everyone how great this dress is looking.

"Mami says it's time to practice Party Scene." Manuel is standing in the doorway, hanging on to the knob.

I jump, missing a stitch and poking myself with the needle. I didn't even hear Manuel coming.

"Tell her I'm almost done with this dress."

"¡Vamos!" I hear my mom shouting downstairs, clapping her hands to gather everyone together.

"She said now."

I groan and stand up, shaking out the dress and draping it back over the chair. It's so pretty, and I wonder which of my friends will get to wear this dress.

Downstairs, my mom has roped basically the whole house

into practicing with me. There's Regina's friends, Bridgit who is in Flowers this year (must be weird to be in the *corps de ballet* when your friend is the lead), and Cassadie, who doesn't even do ballet. Álvaro and Yolanda jump in too, but I notice that they're standing far away from each other, and they choose different partners. I wonder if they've talked more about Álvaro moving to New York permanently.

"I'll be with Regina," Yolanda says, grabbing Regina's hand. They take their places to play kids in Party Scene. Álvaro scowls and strolls over to Bridgit, who giggles. I think she's excited to be dancing with a handsome teenager, especially one who's about to dance a solo at the Met. Cassadie plays Manuel's partner and my dad plays my partner, even though in the actual performances he'll play one of the parents. My mom directs everyone. We make a pretty silly-looking Party Scene, with grown-ups playing kids and everyone being such different heights.

There's a lot of acting in Party Scene, and at first it's actually fun pretending that I'm at a party with Regina and all her friends. During the March, my dad lifts me up off the floor for some of the jumps. It feels a little bit like flying. Greg is nice, but I wish my dad could always dance alongside me.

Then the music shifts to the Grandfather Dance, and everyone runs into place. It turns out that even with my dad as my partner, I can't hop-step without landing on someone's toes, on the wrong beat.

"Ow, Sofía!" Bridgit complains, rubbing her foot. "I have to dance with these feet!"

"Sorry," I mumble.

Just then the doorbell rings and Manuel runs to answer it. My mom goes to the window and waves to Eva and Jonah's dad, who drives away as soon as the twins are in the door.

Eva crosses her arms when she sees us lined up in two neat rows in the living room. "What are you all *doing*?" she asks suspiciously. From her tone, you would guess she was the babysitter instead of the teeniest eight-year-old ever.

"Dancing," my mom says cheerily. "How about you and Jonah try? You would *love* going to ballet school with Manuel, Eva. Look, we're jumping." She demonstrates a perfect hop-step.

Eva wrinkles her nose. "No thank you," she says. "Let's go outside." She grabs Manuel by the elbow and Jonah by the wrist. They follow her like two little puppy dogs.

Regina and I look at each other. I can tell she's thinking what I'm thinking: Why does Manuel let Eva boss him around like that? I wonder if I should have told Regina about Ms. Linski calling him Emmanuel.

My mom shakes her head. "Esos niños," she says.

"Unos malcriados," my dad agrees.

My mom claps her hands like she's teaching. "Okay, everybody, break time. Regina, you and your friends go work on place cards for Thanksgiving. We have a lot of people this year! Sofía, vamos a meterle mano a ese hop-step."

"But I always do the place cards!" I decorate them and use calligraphy-like handwriting. My mom knows that.

"I know, but Regina and her friends can do it this time. You and I are going to practice," my mom says.

Before I get very far complaining, everyone else is nowhere to be found and I'm standing there hop-stepping for my mom like I did with Mrs. Jansen. But the more I try to do it right, the worse it seems to get. It's awkward having my mom watch me. I know that being a performing arts teacher is her job, but I've never really seen her *being* a performing arts teacher before. Usually she's the one encouraging other parents to participate in *The Nutcracker,* or cooking, or telling Manuel and his friends to stop being comemierdas, which is what my mom says when kids are annoying her. Right now I feel like a bug being watched by a scientist as my mom paces around me, trying to figure out why her middle child can't master the hop-step her other two got no problem.

When my mom stops the music, I plop down, right there in the middle of the floor. "Everyone is so mean to me now, just because I can't do one little hop-step."

"Like who?" My mom is looking at her phone, which was playing *Nutcracker* music a minute ago.

"Regina is always forcing me to practice when I want to play with my friends, and Abdul made fun of me for bumping into him!"

My mom sets down her phone. "I heard from Mrs. Jansen that your friend Stella showed a lot of grit and determination getting into Level Five. Maybe you could talk to her about practicing."

"I don't want to talk to Stella about practicing! She's always trying to be best friends with Tricia." I almost tell my mom about Stella marking steps with her tongue between her teeth.

"Sofía," my mom says testily, "maybe she's trying to be friends with *you*, too."

I hadn't thought of that. But when I think about Stella, I'm annoyed at her for being another perfect ballet dancer like my sister and my brother, like everyone else but *me*.

I feel so crummy I'm about to cry, but that just bugs my mom. "Sofía. Hazme el favor. Everyone has been trying to *help* you, and you've been goofing off."

"I'm helping too! I'm doing the beads for Regina's costumes! Don't you remember?"

"Your job is not to decorate costumes. Your job is to do what your dance teacher tells you to do and practice the hop-step every day."

It doesn't even matter how hard I've been working to make *The Nutcracker* beautiful. My mom thinks I'm goofing off no matter what I do.

"Do you want to get up and try it again?"

I stand and mutter under my breath, "You never make Regina practice at home."

My mom hears me. "Sofía Carmen," she says, her tone white-hot now. "Las comparaciones son odiosas. You are not your sister."

"Yeah, she can do whatever she wants and I have to practice."

"Sofía, ¿tú sabes cuánto yo quisiera tener a mis hermanas cerca?"

I really put my foot in it now. I should have just kept my mouth shut, but it's not *fair* how Regina and Manuel are ballet stars and everyone thinks that I just "goof off" and don't care at all. Now my mom is on about how she doesn't live near her sisters, which for some reason means *I* have to be super nice to Regina. I think it would be better if my mom just went to visit her sisters more often, instead of breathing down my neck about being nice to *my* sister.

And besides, I *am* nice. I'm sewing for her.

My mom is scrolling on her phone now, fiercely swiping her thumb against the screen like mini-*frappés*. She does this whenever she's mad at me—she'll just take out her phone and use it to ignore me. While she angry-swipes, I practice the hop-step silently on my own. It's boring. It's not like being at a party at all. I imagine *The Nutcracker* is actually a show about these twisted Victorian people who torture their guests every year at Christmas. Without meaning to, I giggle.

My mom clears her throat. "You know, ballet is very important to our family, Sofía."

I bite my lip, resisting the urge to retort, in my most sarcastic tone, "You don't say."

"Without ballet, Papi and I would have never made it to the United States. We would be living in Cuba, and you and Regina and Manuel wouldn't be living in a house like this, with every toy and snack and activity you could ever want at your fingertips. You understand that, right?"

"Yes."

"You are *very* lucky, Sofía."

"I know that."

"Other people don't have what we have. Look at Mrs. Lewis, entertaining you and driving you around all day. She must think you're some princess, living in a big place like this."

I'm a little surprised, because our house is actually kind of small. Regina and I have to share a room, and our guests always end up in the living room or the attic or even in our rooms, with Manuel sleeping on the floor. If we had a huge house like Tricia's, everyone could have their own room.

My mom must see the confusion in my face, because she goes on. "Sí, señorita. Did you know that Mike and Jessie and Mrs. Lewis all share a one-bedroom apartment? If she can find time to help everyone even when her sister is in the hospital, *you* can find time to practice."

I say nothing. I try to remember how I acted shopping with Mrs. Lewis. Was I being a princess? Did I brag about our house? I didn't know it was that big. Did Mrs. Lewis think I spent a lot of money on ribbons and lace and beads? I thought we were having a good time, talking about colors and what would look good with each dress, but maybe Mrs. Lewis thought I was just a silly spoiled brat. I keep my eyes on my feet.

"Y además," my mom goes on, "you're not thinking about Yolanda and Álvaro. What *they* are going through. Yolanda was a principal ballet dancer and Álvaro has won ballet awards. But it's *still* difficult for them. If your papi and I hadn't come to the United States when we did—"

I want to cover my ears. It's like listening to Laurita, but with the volume turned up to one hundred and ten. My mom's going to tell me about the backlog, about how Laurita's grandmother might die in the Dominican Republic, about how Cubans cross the border like everyone else now, about how if my parents hadn't been ballet dancers and gotten out of Cuba at the exact right moment . . . My chest is going to explode, and all I can think is—

"¡Y tú! ¡Quejándote por un hop-step!"

"OKAY!" I burst out. "I get it. I'll learn the hop-step, I promise. You can throw out all my stuff if you want. Just— stop. Stop!" I run up the stairs, wiping my eyes and ignoring my mom, who is still calling my name when I yank open the door to my bedroom and dive into bed.

CHAPTER EIGHTEEN

"Sofía?" Regina comes into our room and closes the door behind her.

I bury my head deeper into my pillow and don't look up. "Aren't Bridgit and Cassadie still here?"

"They had to go do homework. School tomorrow."

Right. School.

"Mami told me to come check on you. She said you were being majadera."

I sit up. "I was not! She just kept telling me all this horrible stuff about Cuba and Mrs. Lewis all because I can't learn the hop-step!" I wipe my nose on the back of my hand.

Regina sits down on the bed and rubs my back. I cuddle against her shoulder. "Mami just wants you to understand," she says. "She doesn't want you to take anything for granted."

"I don't."

"You know how Mami is. She's always had to work twice as hard as everyone else—just to *get* to the United States, she had to be this amazing ballet dancer. And she works harder at the high school than every other teacher—you know that."

I do know that. When the high school has its big musical performance in the spring, she stays later than anyone, making sure each kid has extra time to practice.

"It's so unfair. Why do we have to do everything so *perfect*"—I spit out the word—"just to have the same things as everyone else in Pine Hill?"

Regina laughs. "And we're the lucky ones. We get to live in Pine Hill."

I think about Mrs. Lewis, and what my mom said about how she can't find a bigger place. My heart feels so heavy.

"You know why," Regina goes on.

And I do know why, I think I've known why my entire life, except I never really paid attention before.

Regina sighs. "A girl at school told me last week that I only got cast as Dewdrop because I'm Latina."

"WHAT?" I straighten up. "Who?"

"You don't know her," Regina says. "She didn't go to Pine Hill Elementary. She says Mrs. Jansen was probably just trying to 'diversify' and there aren't enough Latinas in Pine Hill for her to have picked someone else."

I'm fuming. "That is not okay! I *hate* the things people say—" I want to tell Regina about kids calling Manuel Emmanuel, but I remember how he wanted it to be a secret.

"It's stupid," Regina says. "I know that's not why Mrs. Jansen picked me. But it still made me feel like I'd better be extra good."

"You'd better be," I say, crossing my arms. "Otherwise they'll think Mrs. Jansen picked you to make up for how bad your sister is."

Regina giggles. I scowl at her. I can make jokes, but it's too soon for her.

"Oh, come on," Regina says. "It's pretty funny when you step on people's toes."

I narrow my eyes.

"You just need a little bit of practice, Sof. Come on. Just this one performance. It's important to our family."

I stare straight ahead, but I nod slowly. I want to prove to everyone that the Acostas deserve what we get. I want to be *good* in Party Scene.

"Regina?" I ask after a long while. "Are Yolanda and Álvaro going to be—okay? Mami said something."

"Of course they're okay. Mami just worries. She worries that this trip is too expensive for them, and she worries about what will happen to them when they go back."

I choose my words carefully, since I don't want to give away Álvaro's secret. "Like, what could happen to them when they go back?"

Regina waves her hand airily. "Nothing. Mami's just paranoid. It's hard to live in Cuba. Don't you remember when we visited?"

I remember that Yolanda lived in a big house that was broken into lots of different apartments. I remember how the air smelled like diesel fuel and how we spent a lot of time waiting on lines: lines for the grocery store, lines to get our cell phones set up, lines to get cash to buy those things in the first place.

"Mami just worries that things are going to be tough for Yolanda when she goes back. Álvaro's going to join the Ballet Nacional de Cuba, and he'll have to travel a lot. Yolanda can't go with him on every trip—this one was only because Yolanda got special permission—and Mami thinks she's going to be lonely after this."

I suck in my breath sharply. Wait until everyone finds out that Álvaro is going to move to New York City and join ABT. Then they'll all be *really* worried about Yolanda.

"But Mami will make sure she's okay," I say quickly.

Regina smiles. "She'll find a way to take care of her friend."

I think more about our trip to Cuba, and Yolanda being in that cut-up house alone. Everything about Cuba was different— I remember decorative tiles on the ground, and how I wanted to take pictures of all the designs. It didn't make sense to me. My parents kept talking about when they lived in Cuba, but to me, my parents live *here*. In *our* house, in Pine Hill.

When we left, my mom said that we would be back the next year. But the thing about Cuba is, you can't just go. Because of the embargo, the United States doesn't make it easy to visit Cuba. You have to fill out lots of paperwork, and there aren't always good flights, the way there are when we go see our family in Puerto Rico. Once we had to fly to Canada before flying to Cuba, even though Canada is the opposite direction. It's even harder for my family, because my parents were born in Cuba but we were born in the United States, and the two countries want different permissions. I hope Regina's right, that my mom can take care of Yolanda even when she's far away. Because now that Yolanda's been to New York and we've gone shopping together and she's *my* friend too, it hurts to think about her being alone.

Regina rubs my back some more. "Yolanda and Álvaro are going to be fine. And in the meantime, we have to enjoy their visit. Álvaro's going to introduce us to ABT people!"

I know I'm way too young to go meet dancers in New York City with teenagers, and anyway I don't think any ABT people are going to be interested in a fifth grader who can't even hop-step. But Regina including me feels like a warm hug, and I squeeze her tightly. I wish there were a way I could hang on to my sister, a way to stop her from joining ABT and becoming a famous ballerina, from leaving me behind.

In the evening, I creep downstairs, carrying a pillowcase full of art supplies and other odds and ends. I pause in the stairwell leading to the first floor. From this spot, I can hear the annoying beeps of Manuel in the living room, playing a game on one of my parents' phones. In the kitchen, my mom is making dinner, humming *The Nutcracker* while she does, and my dad is typing away on his laptop.

The basement door is at the bottom of the stairs in between the kitchen and the living room. I slip through it without anyone seeing me. In my spot next to the boiler, I unload the pillowcase: the Ariel doll Tricia grabbed, a scrap of fabric that's half sewn into a curtain for our cardboard theater, a Barbie doll I was supposed to throw away last year but have been using as a model, and a bunch of other things I have been hiding in the closet in my bedroom and working on whenever Regina is out with her friends or at rehearsal. I tuck everything neatly under the stairs, then give Jingle, Solarie, and Mr. Rumpkins each a squeeze in turn.

"I might not be here for a while," I whisper to them. "I have too much practice to do. But I'll be back after *The Nutcracker*." I bury my nose in Mr. Rumpkins's fur, then put him back in his spot and head upstairs.

In the dining room, I take a deep breath. I lift my right foot up and hop backward. My left foot is a little too slow, and my feet don't land together. I take another deep breath. Maybe if my feet can meet in the air, they'll land together too. I try that. It's almost impossible. I do it ten times in a row, stumbling or landing too far back each time. I'm glad everyone is busy and no one can see me mess up. I keep practicing, hop-step, hop-step, hop-step, until my dad calls "¡A la mesa!" and it's time to go eat.

CHAPTER NINETEEN

Tricia, Stella, Abdul, and I are all at Stella's house, gathered around her tablet watching a video of last year's *Nutcracker*. Stella had the idea of having practice at her house before our real rehearsal at Mrs. Jansen's. I kind of wish Tricia could have just come to my house like a normal Saturday, but I can use all the help I can get, so here I am. We talk about our Party Scene dresses and I tell them about the trim I'm adding. Everyone is really excited.

It's hard to see the dancers in the tablet because there are a lot of people on the stage and the screen is so small. Plus, Abdul keeps asking us to zoom in on the person who was in his spot last year, so we can't see the whole stage. Luckily, Stella is *determined*. She must have watched the video a thousand times before. We let Abdul practice his part in front of the tablet while Stella helps Tricia and me.

It turns out it's a lot easier to learn from Stella than it is from Mrs. Jansen or my parents. I'm not sure why, but it's easier with just three of us there. Apparently putting her tongue between her teeth while she focuses also gives Stella eyes in the back of her head, because even when she's demonstrating in front of Tricia and me, she seems to notice when I mess something up. When she corrects me, I don't think about how terrible I am at dancing or how I don't belong in the Acosta family; I just look at my feet and do what Stella told me to do. I didn't even realize it, but every time Mrs. Jansen corrects me at ballet, I know she must be thinking that I'm such a disappointment compared to Regina. It turns out it's a lot harder to learn a dance that way.

After we practice for a while, Stella's mom brings out a tray of ballet-slipper-shaped sugar cookies. They're perfectly baked, golden around the edges, with a light dusting of glitter sprinkles. We each have a glass of milk to go with them. There's a stack of paper napkins on the edge of the tray, and Tricia takes one, unfolds it, and spreads it across her lap as if we were at a fancy restaurant and not sitting on the floor of Stella's family room.

Abdul rolls his eyes. "Is this your Modern Manners stuff again?"

Stella folds a napkin across her lap. "Don't make fun of her. This is really what you're supposed to do, every time you eat."

Abdul grabs a napkin and dramatically shakes it out, then drapes it over his head. "Like this?"

I burst out laughing, and Tricia and Stella do too. Tricia

whacks him with the cookie in her hand, and it breaks in half. Abdul grabs the pieces from the floor and jams them into his mouth, which is mostly hidden by the napkin on his head.

"Mmmm," Abdul says, "delicious. I'm so glad I used my Modern Manners to cover my mouth—the *proper* way."

We all howl. I'm laughing so hard the sides of my cheeks hurt. When everyone calms down and Abdul has taken the ridiculous napkin off his head, I finally get around to asking, "What are Modern Manners?"

Tricia and Stella look at each other. After a minute, Tricia clears her throat. "It's not a big deal. Just this class Stella and I are doing for a few weeks."

I'm taken aback. Tricia and I always do the same activities. "Is it after school?" I ask. "Can I sign up?"

Again, Tricia and Stella look at each other, as if they're parents waiting to tell a kid some bad news. I should have been prepared for what comes next.

"Technically," Tricia says, "it's a class for members of the country club only."

Stella's face is bright red, and Tricia starts brushing the glitter sprinkles off her cookie and into her napkin, as if she's determined to scrape them all off.

"Oh."

"It's not that big a deal," Tricia says in a rush. "It's just a few weeks—we'll be done with it before you know it."

Stella taps her hand to my shoulder, like she's not sure

what she wants to do. "We can invite you to the party at the end. Everyone can bring a guest."

"It's not that fun anyway," Tricia adds. "You just learn stuff like how to do napkins properly."

I stare at my lap. My napkin is folded up on my knee. I haven't really touched it. There are crumbs on my pants. I wonder if I've been doing everything wrong all along. I guess only country club kids get to find out.

That evening I sit on the front steps of my house and watch the sky turn wispy and gray. Across the street, Laurita comes out of her house, crunching dead leaves with her sneakers and tossing a ball to herself. After a few minutes, she notices me sitting on my steps and crosses the street.

"Catch!" she calls, and throws the ball toward me. Instinctively, I reach out and grab it in my gloved hands. My gloves are wool and they aren't grippy like baseball mitts, so the ball slides a bit, but I hang on to it. I toss the ball back to Laurita. She catches it easily in one hand and climbs up the steps. "Hey, what's your family doing for Thanksgiving?" she asks.

I bury my face in my hands. I had forgotten Thanksgiving was next week. "Ugh," I complain. "*The Nutcracker* is only two weeks after Thanksgiving and I have to learn the hop-step *and* finish the Party Scene costumes."

"Don't forget Mr. Fallon's party. Right before Christmas."

"Oh, geez." I had forgotten about the party. And we have Álvaro's big performance at the Met. I promised Laurita I would go look at the Acorn Corners construction site to get some information for our exhibit, but I haven't been anywhere near there.

"We should probably work on our project more."

"Yeah."

Laurita leans back on the step like she lives here. "What's wrong?"

I sigh. "You know how everyone in my family is an amazing dancer?"

Laurita rolls her eyes. "I've heard."

"Well, I'm not. I can't learn this one step in Party Scene and it's messing up the whole *Nutcracker*."

"I seriously doubt one dance is messing up the whole *Nutcracker*."

I tell Laurita how Mrs. Jansen says that the people at ABT are going to take the entire show into account when they see Regina's audition video, not just her performance of Dewdrop.

"That's not true," Laurita says flatly. "She's just pushing you. My travel coach says stuff like that sometimes. Tells us there are scouts coming to games or whatever. They just want us to work harder."

I put my hands between my knees. "Yeah, but—" I try to explain. "Being good at ballet is like the whole reason my family gets to live in the United States. And Regina's going to become a famous ballerina someday—everyone knows it." I swallow hard. "She's going to travel the world. Our friends say everyone is going to throw open their doors to her because of dance. If I can't do ballet, where will I be?"

"You'll still be her sister."

I shake my head. "Remember what you said? About country clubs?" I almost tell Laurita about Modern Manners, but I don't. She would probably laugh that I even *want* to go to Modern Manners.

Laurita nods.

"It's like that. If I'm good at ballet, it makes up for not being the type of family that goes to the country club. It's like I have to *earn* living in Pine Hill by being special, and if I stink at ballet, I don't deserve it. I'm just like any other immigrants' kid, then."

"You shouldn't have to be great at dance for your rich friends to include you," Laurita says. "*I'm* an immigrants' kid and I'm not a dancer. Does that mean you think *I* don't deserve to live here?"

"Well, no, it's different for you. I mean, my family—"

"Do you think your mom really cares whether you're a famous ballet dancer?"

"She seemed pretty sure during hop-step practice."

"I bet she just doesn't want you to give up. Like how my mom always makes me stick out softball to the end of the season even if I don't like the team that year."

"Maybe," I mutter.

Laurita shakes her head. "It's stupid to think you have to be some kind of star to belong in Pine Hill. I mean, look at my abuela. She can barely walk, but I still think she should get to move here."

"Of course she should!"

"So, it's the same for you. You don't have to be a ballet genius to live here. Geez. This is why the exhibit is important for Mr. Fallon's party."

"Why?"

"So people get that we have to be nicer to immigrants, and not just to the ones who are famous." Laurita tosses the ball down the steps, sprints down to catch it, and keeps going all the way home.

CHAPTER TWENTY

I have so many dresses piled in my arms as I walk into Mrs. Jansen's Ballet Academy that I can barely see, and Manuel has to hold open the doors for me. It's the last practice before Thanksgiving, and it's the day we're trying on our costumes for Party Scene. Manuel and I walk straight past the costume closet and into the little studio, where everyone is waiting. Mrs. Lewis has rolled in the costume rack with the boys' Party Scene costumes, and she's standing next to it with a measuring tape around her neck and a clipboard in her hands. After Thanksgiving, our next practice will be a dress rehearsal at the theater, so Mrs. Lewis is assigning everyone their costumes today. Mrs. Jansen is in the corner, giving Carrie, who is playing Clara, some one-on-one pointers.

My smile falters as I approach Mrs. Lewis. I haven't seen her since my mom said that about my possibly being a brat. But Mrs. Lewis smiles encouragingly at me and holds out her arms.

"Let's see those dresses, baby girl."

I pass them to her and she grips all the hangers in one strong arm and hoists them onto the costume rack. She whistles. "You went all out, Sofía!"

I try not to look too pleased with myself and raise my shoulders as if to say, "It was nothing." But really, I'm so proud of the dresses. They look almost new, and I did all that sewing while also practicing Party Scene for an hour every morning.

Mrs. Jansen looks up from Carrie's feet, which she was adjusting. "You did that, Sofía?"

I nod proudly, but to my surprise, Mrs. Jansen frowns. "You're supposed to be focusing on improving your dancing." She turns to Mrs. Lewis. "I said she could help, but she can't be distracted from rehearsals right now. Could we keep her on task?"

I want to shrink into the costume rack and never be seen again. Half the people in the room heard Mrs. Jansen. Abdul and Zack stopped running around, and Tricia and Stella both have their mouths hanging open.

I try to clear my throat to shout that I have been *very* focused and practicing every day, but nothing comes out.

Mrs. Lewis doesn't say much to Mrs. Jansen. She just replies "We'll stay on track!" in a chipper voice and turns back to the costume rack. "Okay, kids," she announces. "Everyone line up for their fitting."

There's some pushing and shoving now, because everyone

wants to be first in line to try on one of the gorgeous dresses I helped decorate.

The first few dresses go quickly. The most ornate dress, in a deep crimson, is for Carrie, since she plays Clara. Dahlia takes the smallest one, and that leaves Tricia, Stella, and me. Stella is a little taller than Tricia and me, so Mrs. Lewis assigns her the biggest remaining dress and makes a few notes—she's going to have to take it in so it will fit Stella.

When Mrs. Lewis slips the dress she picks for me over my head, it's like sliding into a heavenly cloud. The inside of the dress is silky and smooth, and the pattern of lavender ribbons and rosettes that I added to the trim makes it sweet and delicate. I admire myself in the mirror, swishing the skirt from side to side, while Mrs. Lewis declares it a perfect fit.

That leaves Tricia with the last remaining dress, a blue one with light green trim. It looks great on Tricia, but when I see her face, I know something is wrong. She's biting her lip and cocking her head to the side while she looks in the mirror. She turns to different angles. It's like she's trying to make her reflection look different than it does. She looks over her shoulder at the costume rack, and suddenly I know what the problem is.

"Mrs. Lewis," I say quickly, "can I switch dresses with Tricia?"

"Hmm? How come? The one you tried fit you fine."

"I liked the trimming on the other dress," I lie. "I remember from when I was sewing it."

"All right then." Mrs. Lewis scratches my name off the list and writes in Tricia's on top. Tricia wriggles out of the blue dress. She doesn't quite meet my eye, but when Mrs. Lewis hands her the dress with the lavender trim, she smiles and runs her hands over the velvet. Lavender is Tricia's favorite color. I should have remembered from the beginning.

During break, Stella and Tricia and I have our lunches in the dressing room.

"Mrs. Jansen's worried, but I've been practicing," I say nervously.

"You're getting better," Tricia says warmly.

"I guess I'll see at rehearsal today."

"At least your dress fits you," Stella says. "Your trim came out great, Sofía, but mine is huge on me."

"Oh, don't worry about that," I reply. "Mrs. Lewis will take it in and you won't even be able to tell. It's so nice of her to help with all the costumes. Mrs. Jansen must be so thankful."

Tricia and Stella exchange glances. "You mean it's nice of Mrs. Jansen to let her volunteer," Tricia says.

"Huh?" That's not what I meant at all, actually.

Tricia sets down her bento box. "Mrs. Lewis doesn't pay the parent fee for *The Nutcracker,* and I don't think she pays for classes for Mike and Jessie, either—my mom contributes to the scholarship fund, so we know."

I'm kind of relieved that Mrs. Lewis isn't spending a whole lot of money on ballet classes, after what my mom told me about their apartment. "Hang on a second," I say. "What parent fee for *The Nutcracker*?" This is the first I'm hearing of it.

"Didn't you read your packet at the audition?" Tricia says. "It was right there at the beginning. There's a form where parents have to say whether they want to pay a fee to have their kid participate in *The Nutcracker* or volunteer to help with costumes and chaperoning and stuff."

Actually, I didn't really look at my packet other than to see I got into Party Scene. My mom took all our packets in the car. I'm pretty sure they said *parent information packet* anyway, not *kid information packet*.

"So, which did your parents pick?"

Stella giggles. "My mom said she would rather walk on hot coals than chase after a bunch of kids backstage."

"Same with my mom," Tricia says. "She would much rather pay the fee. It's nice that Mrs. Jansen has a volunteering option for the scholarship kids."

I wonder whether my parents paid the fee. My mom is always around when we do *The Nutcracker,* but that's because she is in the actual performance—she'll be onstage as a parent with us during Party Scene, and she always sticks around to help the teenagers once we're at the theater, because some of them are her students at the high school. But she's not doing anywhere near as much work as Mrs. Lewis.

I pick at my sandwich. My chest is tight, like something is squeezing on my heart. I think about how much time I spent making all those tiny stitches on the trimming of the dresses.

I think about Mrs. Lewis taking in Stella's dress for her so it won't be too big. I take a deep breath.

"I still think it's really nice of Mrs. Lewis to volunteer. Paying a fee is great if you have money, but sewing is a lot more work. We're really lucky that Mrs. Lewis helps us so much."

Stella bites her lip. "There are a lot of costumes in *The Nutcracker*," she agrees.

Tricia doesn't reply, but as soon as I've spoken up, the squeezing in my chest loosens just enough so I can go into rehearsal with my head held high, ready to show everyone that I can do this hop-step.

My hop-step is okay. I don't step on anyone, but Mrs. Jansen still tells me I'm behind the music a few times. On the car ride home, I try to focus on the music. It's hard to imagine my legs going that fast. Then I hear my mom say something that gets my attention.

"Hang on," I interrupt. "Did you just say Mrs. Lewis is moving?"

"Si Dios quiere," my mom says. "Right near us!"

"No way!" I sit up. "That's awesome. I could go over and do sewing with her whenever I wanted. Where's she moving? Next to Laurita?"

My mom grins. "Haven't you seen that old parking lot by the grocery store? They're building new apartments there."

"Acorn Corners!"

My mom is totally impressed I know about Acorn Corners, and just like I guessed, Manuel is really excited about a construction project. He wants my dad to take him as soon as they start building, but my dad tells us it's going to be a while before they actually build it. The construction company needs to get lots of permits before they can start, and there has to be a town hall meeting where people who already live in Pine Hill say what they think about the building.

"But you should see the design!" my dad says. "It's going to be beautiful. Really spacious apartments."

"Mrs. Lewis is going to put in her application right away," my mom says. "So fingers crossed she'll be moving in next fall."

I toss my ballet slippers into the air triumphantly. "Woohoo!" I shout. "Plus, Jessie and Davy are like the same age. Davy will finally have someone to play with!"

As the car rolls into our driveway, I lean back again, satisfied. I may be behind the music, but at least I might have Mrs. Lewis as a neighbor this time next year.

CHAPTER TWENTY-ONE

I'm standing in the dining room in my ballet slippers early Thanksgiving morning, looking at the place cards Regina and her friends made, thinking about how much my mom is going to regret giving them this job. They basically just folded over fourteen index cards and wrote people's names on them. They didn't use a fancy pen or anything.

The table is sparkling. Last night my mom set everything out so that she wouldn't have to worry about it today. She used her elegant dishes, and her fanciest tablecloth, which was embroidered all over with flowers by my great-aunt Nena in Cuba. Since my parents had to leave most of their stuff behind when they left Cuba, they don't have many special things from older relatives, so we treasure what we do have. We only use Nena's tablecloth for holidays and birthdays. The silverware and the wineglasses catch the dawn light coming in through the windows, and little patterns of rainbows hit the floor and the tablecloth. Everything is perfect, except those place cards. But I turn my back firmly on the table and go to the far corner of the dining room, where I'm safely hidden from sight.

I've been getting up early every morning to practice in the living room before anyone can see me. I've been jerking myself awake as soon as even a little bit of gray creeps in through the windows and lands on my eyelids. It's dark and cold in the house then, before the radiators have started up. I don't like being awake all by myself. But it's easier to practice without my family watching. I can focus on the steps instead of imagining what they're thinking: how this step is so easy they can't believe a fifth grader still can't do it, how I'm going to mess up the whole *Nutcracker,* how no one in the history of the Acosta family has ever failed to master a simple ballet combination and if there were an emergency and we all had to get out of the country to go someplace new and safe, probably I would be the only one not to get a visa. The visa people would say, "We want Regina and Manuel and their parents because they will be beautiful dancers in this new country where there isn't anything bad happening, but Sofía will have to stay behind because we have no use for her in our ballets."

It's very hard to practice the hop-step when you're thinking about what will happen if you get trapped without a visa, so I've been having my own mini-rehearsals alone. I pull on a warm sweater, sneak down the stairs in my ballet slippers, practice a zillion times, and get back upstairs and into bed before the sun comes up and my dad starts singing "¡Al combate, corred, bayameses!"

Today it's a little more complicated, because my tía Rosi and my cousin Roberto flew in from Miami last night. Since Yolanda is already using the attic, Tía Rosi is sleeping in the living room. So I practice the Grandfather Dance in the corner of the dining room, humming the music to myself. I think part of the problem is that even if I manage to get the steps right on my own, when I do them to the actual music, it's hard to move that fast. I make my dancing a little quicker and lighter.

"Buenos días, Sofía Carmen." Tía Rosi is a light sleeper, apparently, because she's awake and standing in the doorway to the dining room. I freeze in place and try to look like I wasn't dancing.

"¿Practicando ya?"

Okay, I guess there's no other way to explain what I'm doing in my ballet slippers at the crack of dawn on a day with no school and no ballet. I shrug like it's no big deal.

Tía Rosi shakes her head. "I can see you're becoming like everyone else in your family," she tells me in Spanish. "Nothing but ballet in that brain of yours."

I laugh and don't say much. It wouldn't be a bad thing if I became more like everyone else.

"¿Te hago café con leche?" Tía Rosi asks, heading into the kitchen. I follow her, nodding my head. I like having café con leche in the morning. Tricia is amazed that I can drink it, because she says coffee just tastes bitter to her and she wouldn't have it even if her parents did let her, but I don't think it tastes bitter. Café con leche the way my family makes it has a lot of milk and sugar. It's more like liquid coffee ice cream, if you ask me. Plus, it makes me feel sophisticated and mature when other people are so impressed that I know how to drink coffee.

Tía Rosi asks me how school is and tells me I have to encourage my cousin Roberto to go back to school. He's working for a cousin's company in Miami right now, but Tía Rosi wants him to finish college. One of the good things about Tía Rosi is that she can keep up a conversation pretty much on her own, so I just let her talk as I sip my café con leche. I pull off my ballet slippers under the table so that everyone won't ask me about them when they come downstairs.

"So when you see him," Tía Rosi goes on, "¡insiste! Okay?"

I agree, even though there's no chance I'm going to tell Roberto what to do. He's nineteen years old! That's a grown-up! Manuel is beside himself with joy that there are now *two* teenagers sleeping in his room. He worships Roberto and would probably sleep on the chimney if it meant he got to hang out with him.

What I really want to ask my tía Rosi is what it's like to be my mom's little sister, and not to be a ballet dancer at all. My mom and Tía Rosi look alike, but Rosi doesn't move the same way as my mom. When she walks, she doesn't glide. It's just walking. When she sits, she plonks down in a chair like everyone else, whereas my mom and Regina melt into chairs. My mom was selected at a special audition to go to ballet school in Cuba when she was a little girl, because she was identified as having exceptional talent. Alicia Alonso herself was there the day my mom auditioned. My mom went on to perform all over the world with the Ballet Nacional de Cuba before moving to the United States, whereas Rosi went to regular school and only got to move to Miami because my mom helped her get permission to come. I wish I could be a hero like my mom, who helps her family and friends get visas. I want to ask my tía Rosi what it's like to be the sister who got help instead of the sister who helped. I want to ask her what it's like to be the sister who doesn't have exceptional talent.

But before I can open my mouth, there's a loud clatter on the steps.

"¡Prima!" Roberto opens his arms wide for a hug. Even though it's early, he has already showered and put on cologne and fresh hair gel. His shirt and pants are crisply ironed, and his gold watch gleams. Manuel is bouncing around next to him, curls flying in every direction. Álvaro shuffles down behind the two of them.

"Can we go to get the chairs now? Can we?" Manuel asks. He turns to me, his face glowing. "I'm going to go with Roberto to pick up extra chairs for Thanksgiving dinner!" Unable to contain his excitement about an outing with Roberto, Manuel *chassés* across the room, flowing into a *tombé, pas de bourré*, warming up with a *glissé*, and leaping into a perfect *sauté* with both legs extended in an aerial split. I am seriously impressed. I didn't know Manuel could get that kind of elevation. I've seen my dad do that, but Manuel is only eight!

"¡Así se hace!" Álvaro says, praising Manuel.

Roberto frowns. "Manuel, too, with the ballet?"

I roll my eyes. It's the same old boys-can't-do-ballet thing, and it's totally not true. Half of the dancers at ballet companies are men, and anyone who thinks ballet isn't athletic enough for men can find me at 5:30 a.m. for some hop-step practice.

But the question is directed at me, so I shrug. "He's really good."

"If people saw a man doing that in Miami, you don't want to know the names they would call him," Roberto says.

Álvaro raises an eyebrow, but he doesn't say anything.

"The men at Miami City Ballet seem to do pretty well," I reply coolly. There was just a profile on one of their male principal dancers in *Dance Magazine*. I read the whole thing. "And hey," I say to Roberto defensively. "My *dad* was a ballet dancer—are you going to call him names?"

"Nothing I can do about your dad now," Roberto says. He sizes up Álvaro, taking in his lanky legs and precise posture, then shakes his head. "But my little cousin? I should be teaching him to do some real guy stuff."

I bite my lip and hope Manuel can't hear Roberto. But Manuel stops dancing suddenly, and I know he has heard. He doesn't say anything, but he walks over to the kitchen table and sits down, his back held very upright. I wonder what he's thinking and try to catch his eye, but he ignores me. By the time Roberto has had his coffee and gotten the keys to my dad's car, Manuel seems to have forgotten about it. As they walk out the door, Manuel listens rapturously while Roberto tells him about his car in Miami, and how he cleans and waxes it and takes care of it as if it were a precious baby. Still, I can't help noticing that Manuel's not exactly leaping across the driveway, and Álvaro hasn't moved toward the coffee. He's just standing there, watching them go.

When the rest of the grown-ups wake up, it's like the Thanksgiving party has already started. Regina is the only person in the house who's still sleeping, but the adults are having coffee and pastries in the living room and laughing at every little thing. I hold my café con leche with both hands and go up to Álvaro, who's leaning against the kitchen counter and staring into space.

"I'm sorry about my cousin. He's the worst."

"People think like that," Álvaro says glumly. "That's life as an artist." He reaches for a spoon and adds some sugar to a mug, making himself a second café con leche.

"Just wait until—" I almost said "you're a famous ABT dancer," but then I stop to think. It's like what Laurita said. How unfair is it that Álvaro has to be famous just for Roberto to keep his mouth shut?

But Álvaro knows what I was about to say. He leans back

and glances into the living room, where the adults are still talking loudly. They're not about to take a breath anytime soon.

"I don't know if I'm going to take the job," he says.

"What? You have to. It's *ABT*," I whisper, taking a peek at the living room myself.

"You saw how people will treat me," Álvaro says. "If that's how other Cubans are going to see me, what's everyone else going to say?"

"You can*not* let Roberto stop you from moving to New York! He only visits once a year."

"It's not just that," Álvaro explains. "I have to find a place to live. Ballet dancers don't make that much money. You have to get pretty famous, get people to sponsor you and all, before you can make a good living in the United States. I can't stay in your brother's room forever."

I make a face. "Manuel would be *thrilled* if you lived in his bedroom forever."

Álvaro cracks a smile, but it's not enough. Then I snap my fingers. "I've got a great idea! They're building a new apartment in Pine Hill, right down the road from us. It's called Acorn Corners, and the apartments aren't going to be too expensive. You could live there, come here for dinner every night, and take the train into the city!"

"Oh?" Álvaro stirs his café con leche.

"I'm serious! It's the perfect plan." I punch his arm jokingly. "Until you're ABT-famous," I add. "Then you'll prob-ably live in a fancy New York City skyscraper and forget all about us little people. I mean, except Regina. She'll live in a bigger skyscraper and be an even more famous soloist."

Álvaro throws his head back and finally drinks some of his café con leche. "Regina is some dancer, that's for sure." He wipes the milk froth off his mouth. "Thanks for the Acorn Corners tip." He punches my shoulder back. "It would be fun being your neighbor—until I get my skyscraper, that is."

CHAPTER TWENTY-TWO

Later that morning, Roberto pulls my dad's car all the way up to the back of the house and everyone helps unload the extra chairs. There's a sharp hint of frost in the air, and I'm bundled up in my puffy coat. The sky is gray, and most of the trees have lost their leaves, but there's one in Davy's yard that has been holding on, orange and yellow against the chalky sky.

Suddenly, my mom comes running up the driveway, flapping her arms and shouting.

"¡Hay que poner la mesa!"

"Ma, calm down," Regina says. "We did the table last night, remember?"

"No!" my mom yells. "We have to *redo* the table!"

Maybe she finally realized that it was a mistake to have Regina make the place cards.

Everyone looks at her blankly, and my mom takes a deep breath. "I just saw Mrs. Sánchez, and she and her family don't have any plans for Thanksgiving. No one coming. She didn't even buy a turkey. She was feeling sorry about her mom—this is our neighbor," she explains to Tía Rosi. "Her mom is stuck in the DR and they've been trying to move her here, ya tú sabes, todo un lío—and she didn't feel up to cooking."

Regina clears her throat. "Ma, what does Mrs. Sánchez's mom have to do with the table?"

My mom throws her arms up in the air. "That's just what I have been trying to tell you. I invited her here. And she was so happy! She's coming with her husband and Laurita. That will be great for Sofía." My mom beams at me like she's just made personal arrangements with Santa Claus for Christmas to come early.

In the end, we all pitch in to get the table reset with extra place settings, and the Sánchez place cards are extra special, since thankfully we all agree that it would be a little tragic to let Regina make three more. The table looks beautiful, even if it will be hard to get in and out once everyone is sitting down.

"Acosta Accordion: HUGEST setting," Davy announces when he walks in for Thanksgiving dinner. He's coming through the front door for a change, and with both of his parents, which is an even bigger change. But he ditches them right away and goes to "help" my mom and Tía Rosi in the kitchen, which mostly involves Davy spilling rice everywhere. But my mom just says "Más se perdió en la guerra" and sweeps it all up.

Davy is right about the hugest setting; by three in the

afternoon there are so many people in our house it feels like it's throbbing with all the noise of everyone talking and the Cuban music my parents play loudly through the speakers. My dad is deep in conversation with Laurita's dad, and my mom and Yolanda and Rosi are with Mrs. Sánchez and Alejandro and Teresa, two of our neighbors who are from Puerto Rico and are asking lots of questions about my aunt Aldema. Regina is talking to Roberto as if she were twenty years old, trying to draw Álvaro, who looks kind of sullen, into the conversation. Manuel is playing phone games with Davy, who is too little to really know how to play them, but that doesn't seem to bother either of them.

I'm standing with Laurita, wondering what we should talk about. Laurita has her mitt on and is bouncing a ball lightly in it, even though I heard her mom telling her as they were coming up the steps that she had to put that away and cut it out before she got to our house because she might break something. I guess Mrs. Sánchez doesn't know about the "Más se perdió en la guerra" rule.

"Hey, you know what?" I ask Laurita.

"Yeah?"

"I know someone who applied to move into Acorn Corners! Mrs. Lewis, from my ballet school." I can tell Laurita is as happy as I hoped she would be. I wish I could tell her about Álvaro. I want her to know that I thought about how she said that no one should have to be a famous star just to belong, and how much it helps knowing that there's going to be somewhere in Pine Hill that Álvaro could afford to live. But a secret is a secret, so instead I ask Laurita if she wants to see my room.

Laurita is more than happy to go somewhere the grown-ups can't see her tossing her ball. Once we get to my and Regina's room, she points to the Dewdrop costume laid across my bed.

"Whoa. What is that?"

I hold it up. "It's Regina's for *The Nutcracker*. The beads and rhinestones were falling off, so I'm fixing it. See?" I point out some of the loose threads in the costume. "I'm replacing them with these."

Laurita takes the round tin from me. She slides the tin side to side to see how the sparkly decorations look when the sunlight hits them. "Cool. You must be really good at sewing if they let you work on Regina's costume."

I settle on my bed with the costume on one knee and take the tin back from Laurita. "I already did the Party Scene dresses, and they look *so* pretty. Someday I want to redo the whole costume closet." I thread a thin needle and fish around for a rhinestone. "I have some other fabric and beads if you want to make something. My parents got me a lot of supplies for costumes, so I have like every craft thing under the sun now. Want to go look?"

I'm half standing up, but Laurita shakes her head. She's doing an imaginary pitch—not throwing the ball, of course, but winding up and checking for the runner over her shoulder. "That's okay. I'm not really a craft person."

If Tricia were here, she would definitely want to make

something from my stash. But it's kind of fun to sit on my bed and sew while Laurita plays imaginary softball. I ask her about her team, and she tells me a hilarious story about her coach. The kids come from all over our county, not just Pine Hill, and Laurita gets to go to different towns and get ice cream after games.

"Your team sounds *fun*. Ballet rehearsals are so strict."

"Isn't there, like, a sewing club you could join instead?" Laurita asks.

I smooth out the Dewdrop costume, savoring the silkiness of the shimmery white fabric. "Not really. There are art classes, I guess. But I'd never have time with ballet and rehearsals and everything."

Laurita looks at my sewing setup: beads and trim all over my bed, a pencil case full of scissors and pins, a chair to drape my creations so they don't get wrinkled. "You could make your own club."

I laugh. "Maybe someday. First I have to do Party Scene in this year's *Nutcracker*. I've *almost* got it all down."

When we sit down at the table, I load up on black beans, rice, and plantains and listen to the grown-ups' conversation about Álvaro's performance at the Met. Laurita's parents, Mr. and Mrs. Sánchez, promise to get tickets.

"It's a big honor," my mom is explaining. "To be selected to dance in a tribute to Alicia Alonso."

"Oh, right, the communist ballerina," Mr. Sánchez says.

There's an awkward silence. The way people in the United States talk, it's like communists all have devil horns coming out of their heads. This is weird for my family. My parents are glad that they live in the United States now, but they're still *Cuban*. Álvaro starts wolfing down rice and beans, and Yolanda's back grows even taller and straighter than usual.

"Alicia Alonso was a *prima ballerina assoluta*," my mom says stiffly. "Dance transcends political boundaries."

Mr. Sánchez chuckles. "Yeah, but the communists sure got a lot of credit for that ballet company of hers, didn't they? I heard she practically trapped dancers in Cuba." He turns toward Álvaro as if he's asking about the weather. "Is it easier for people to get out now?"

My mom coughs into her napkin. I've never seen her so taken aback by a guest before. Usually my mom can handle any social situation. But I think about what she told me about leaving Cuba, and how the hardest part was how Alicia was mad at her, and I wonder: Had Alicia tried to trap *my* parents in Cuba because their dancing helped the communist government? Is that why Alicia was so mad when my parents told her they were moving to the United States? When my mom told me she never spoke to Alicia again, I assumed it was because Alicia was so sad to say goodbye to my parents and wanted them to dance with the Ballet Nacional de Cuba forever because—well, I guess I always imagined that Alicia loved my parents, almost like she was another grandmother

I never met. I didn't realize that Alicia might have been mad that my mom was leaving communism.

"The Ballet Nacional de Cuba hasn't *trapped* anyone," Yolanda says.

Mr. Sánchez chuckles again, and Yolanda looks disgusted.

"Anyway, there's no reason my son would want to leave," Yolanda says, bristling. "He has a bright future in Cuba."

Álvaro takes a giant swig of water and coughs on it. Roberto pounds him on the back, and now Mr. Sánchez gives a big, booming laugh. "I'm sure," he agrees sarcastically.

Mr. Sánchez's words make me see everything differently. I used to think that my parents coming to the United States was about ballet, about finding their fortune and making their dreams come true. I never thought of it as escaping communism. But now Yolanda sputters defensively, and I think about how she and my mom fought when she wouldn't move to the United States after she split from Álvaro's dad. Seeing how angry and red-faced all the adults have suddenly become, I wonder what's really about ballet and what's really about family and what was actually about communism all along.

Regina says daintily, "Alicia Alonso didn't only create the Ballet Nacional de Cuba, Mr. Sánchez. Before she moved home to Cuba, she helped build American Ballet Theatre, right here in New York. George Balanchine created lead parts specifically for her."

George Balanchine was a really important man who practically invented modern-day ballet in the United States. Anyone who even *met* him in the ballet world is low-key famous, so the fact that he created leading roles in his ballets for Alicia Alonso makes her a big deal.

"Balanchine choreographed *Theme and Variations* just for Alicia," Regina says, as if that settles the matter. Also as if *Theme and Variations* is, like, something that everyone knows about. I can tell Mr. Sánchez is losing interest. Sometimes when Regina goes on about ballet for a long time, I get that same glazed-over look on my face.

But my mom is proud of Regina. "See? Alicia Alonso danced ballet in Cuba *and* the United States. She doesn't belong to one country or another. She belongs to art."

I watch the adults' conversation like it's a Ping-Pong match, swiveling my head from person to person to pick up on everything they're saying. When Regina and my mom talk about Alicia Alonso, it's like the line between Cuba and the United States disappears. I want to believe their version of Alicia Alonso, because it makes me think that I don't have to be split all the time—that I don't have to be one way in New York and one way in Cuba. That my family is about something bigger than Cuba versus the United States, communism or leaving.

Then I think something that makes me slump in my chair. There is something bigger and more important, something that unites my family and Yolanda and Álvaro all together, and that something is ballet. But what's the big, important thing if you're not amazing at ballet?

Our neighbor Teresa is trying to smooth things over. "Ballet es como la pelota," she adds. "It doesn't matter if you're Cuban, Dominican, Puerto Rican, or American—we all have baseball in common."

"Exactly!" my dad exclaims, and the next thing I know, he and Mr. Sánchez are deep in conversation about baseball. Laurita leans across the table and joins in, talking animatedly about things like RBIs and whether some guy named Fernández will be sent back to the Dominican Republic if his game doesn't shape up. I don't understand a word of their conversation, but surprisingly, my dad seems to enjoy talking about Cuban baseball as much as he enjoys talking about the Ballet Nacional de Cuba. He's now telling everyone about a game he once saw in Havana. Laurita is hanging on his every word.

My mom turns to Teresa and Mrs. Sánchez and pats Regina on the back. "You know, our Regina might be following Alicia's footsteps to ABT."

Teresa and Mrs. Sánchez immediately start asking Regina lots of questions about her audition for the ABT Summer Intensive, and Regina blushes. When Regina is famous, we're going to have to work on her interview skills. She can't keep turning bright red every time someone asks her about being a prodigy.

After everyone is stuffed, Roberto taps Laurita on the shoulder. He motions to her mitt. "How about a game?"

Laurita jumps up immediately. "Can I go?" she asks her mom.

My mom replies before Mrs. Sánchez can get a word in edgewise. "¡Que vaya a jugar la gente joven! Go ahead and play! You're only young once."

Laurita looks at me. "You coming?"

I have never ever played softball outside of our made-up version that we do at ballet. I'm a little intimidated by how hard and round and not-doll-like Laurita's softball looks. It doesn't look at all soft. I turn to Regina. If she's going, I'll go. But she shakes her head.

"I have to stay safe for Dewdrop," she explains. "I could get injured if I play outside."

Álvaro holds up his hands to say, "Not me," and I'm about to say that I won't play either, but just then Manuel and Davy join us, jumping around Roberto like he's a beanpole they'd like to climb. I remember what Roberto said this morning about teaching Manuel to do guy stuff.

"I'm coming with you all," I announce, and grab my coat from the kitchen hook as we troop out the back door.

It turns out Roberto is not that good at softball, and Laurita has no mercy in taunting him when he swings and misses.

"I'm *ten*!" she shrieks when he strikes out. "That's *half* your age—and you are OUT!"

We had to tweak the rules a bit since we only have five players. We put Roberto and Davy on the same team, figuring that would even them out. But actually Laurita and Manuel and I cream Roberto and Davy. I think Davy is so happy to be included that he doesn't really care, but I can tell Roberto is a little rattled that he can't beat a bunch of kids. I keep one eye on Manuel. Hopefully he's taking an important lesson from this: tough macho cousins aren't any better at sports than other people, they just think they are.

I'm in the outfield when Roberto hits a ball in my direction, and I race backward and jump. It's exhilarating, seeing the white ball almost shining as it zooms across the dark, cold sky. I catch it on the fly and land with both feet together. Laurita cheers and Manuel throws his arms around me. I have never felt better.

"I didn't know you could catch!" Laurita says.

Davy's parents have come to collect him, and Roberto has cried uncle and gone back inside. Manuel is running around the yard on his own, throwing in occasional ballet steps.

"I didn't either! I've never even played softball before."

Laurita grins. "I guess you're just a good Cuban, then."

I laugh. "A good Cuban? Me? You haven't seen me trying to keep the beat at ballet rehearsals. I'm telling you, Alicia Alonso rolls over in her grave every time I move my feet."

"So maybe your Cuban thing isn't ballet. Maybe it's like my Dominican thing: we play pelota!"

Laurita races backward, winds up, and throws the ball to me. I catch it, and as Laurita flashes me a smile and a thumbs-up, I can hardly believe that this person, running around in the dusky air and bursting with joy, is the same girl we once called the Bad News Machine.

CHAPTER TWENTY-THREE

"Sofía!" Regina shouts from the bottom of the stairs. "It's for you!"

"Tell Tricia I'll be down in one second!" I'm tugging on the hem of last year's Easter dress, trying to make it stay straight. I added some sequins and bows to it, and for some reason it's crooked now.

"It's not Tricia!" Regina shouts back.

"What?" I open the door to my room and go to the top of the stairwell so I can see Regina. My dad is standing there too, scowling.

"Niñas," he complains. "¡No se grita!"

"Oh, Papi, we were barely making any noise," Regina retorts. "Sofía has a friend here."

"You shouldn't keep your guests waiting," my dad adds crossly, so I grab a hair ribbon off the desk and head down the stairs. Mrs. Rivera is picking me up in five minutes; I don't know what Laurita is doing here.

Laurita is standing in the living room with a tote bag over her shoulder. I can see the outline of a ball and mitt bulging through the canvas. "What happened to your furniture?" she asks.

I finish tying the ribbon in my hair, hoping the bow is straight. "When we don't have company, we use the living room for ballet practice."

"Huh." Laurita nods at the couch and the stacked-up chairs in the corner. "Cool."

"What are you doing here?" I ask, kind of grouchy, but before Laurita can answer, Álvaro comes into the room.

"¡Qué guapa!" Álvaro says when he sees my dress, and I smile a big smile.

"Do you remember Laurita from Thanksgiving?" I say to him in Spanish. I turn to Laurita, ready to switch into English and reintroduce him, but without missing a beat, Laurita gives Álvaro a kiss on the cheek.

"Qué bueno verte," she says, and for a second I stare at her. I had forgotten that Laurita speaks Spanish too, but it makes sense. Our parents always speak to each other in Spanish.

Then Laurita asks Álvaro if he plays ball, like she's hoping he'll be another Roberto who she can clobber in a game. But Álvaro grins and shakes his curls no. "Yo bailo," he explains. "But I'm not much for baseball."

"Qué pena," Laurita says. She turns to me. "Looks like

you're the only ballplayer around here. But anyway, I wanted to get some work done on the exhibit."

Just then, I hear a car horn honking.

"Sorry, but I gotta go," I say quickly.

"Oh," Laurita says awkwardly. "Where ya going?" she asks nonchalantly.

I shift uncomfortably in my party shoes. "I'm going to the country club." Then, all in a rush, I explain, "Tricia invited me because her Modern Manners class is having their final party today. Everyone's allowed to bring a guest and she picked me."

"Got it. Yeah. Well, you're best friends."

I nod vigorously. "We always invite each other to stuff."

Laurita jerks her head to the door. "You should go, then."

"We're not members," I blurt out. "I'm just a guest."

Laurita shrugs. "Whatever. We can work on the posters later."

"Yeah. Later." I run out the door. Regina will take care of Laurita, I think. Or maybe my mom will give her a sugary snack. That always seems to cheer people up. But just as the door is closing, I sneak one last peek at Laurita. She's still standing in the living room, looking very small in our empty practice space.

The final party for Modern Manners is a Harvest Tea Party theme. I love it. A lot of the kids are grumpy that they have to wear dresses or khakis and leather shoes, but to me everything is magic, almost like being inside a real live Party Scene. We're in an actual ballroom at the country club, and the tables have been set out as if the queen of England were about to show up. Whoever made the place cards used the most elaborate calligraphy I have ever seen. I wonder how long it took them, and if Regina could help me find a YouTube video so I could learn how to do that type of calligraphy.

Tricia and I sit down next to Stella, and we spread our napkins across our laps the way they showed me the other day. Then the servers come out with salads and sandwiches and everyone says thank you. I imagine I'm a lady-in-waiting at a royal castle and chew in very small bites.

Okay, so the food is not that great. The bread kind of tastes like nothing, and there are lots of weird green sprigs and crinkles on absolutely everything. Before long, I'm dreaming of my mom's black beans and rice. I'm imagining how my mom sometimes burns the rice at the bottom a tiny bit, and then it's almost like having crunchy savory rice clusters.

Just when I'm about to bite into my imaginary rice cluster, I hear Stella saying to Jayden from our class at school, "My mom says it's going to be an eyesore."

Jayden shrugs. "That's what my parents said. I just want to keep riding my skateboard."

"Why would you have to stop riding your skateboard?" I ask.

"They're taking away the spare parking lot where I go to ride," Jayden explains.

"They're putting up apartments there," Tricia says. "Didn't you hear?"

My eyes grow wide. "Oh!" I say, a little too loudly. "Yeah, Acorn Corners! I'm really excited because my friend—" I slap my hand to my mouth. I almost gave away Álvaro's secret. I lower my hand and say, more slowly this time, "It will be cool to have some new neighbors."

"Yeah," Tricia replies sarcastically. "Except Jayden can't ride his skateboard and I'm going to have to help my mom carry groceries about a mile every Saturday."

I hadn't thought about that. Most of the time that lot by the grocery store is pretty empty; that's why Jayden rides his skateboard there. It's not even the main grocery store lot—but that one gets so jam-packed on Saturdays that everyone goes to the extra lot. I never really think about it because we live right by the store and walk, but it's way too far from Pine Hill Heights. I've been shopping with Tricia and Mrs. Rivera before. Mrs. Rivera always tells us to close our eyes and visualize a spot. She thinks that will help one appear, but we still end up driving around in circles, looking for a place to park their SUV.

I feel a little bad for Tricia and Mrs. Rivera, and for Jayden's skateboarding, but mostly I'm still excited that Mrs. Lewis and Álvaro might be my new neighbors. Besides, maybe Tricia and her parents could move—the houses in my part of town are smaller, but at least they're closer to the grocery store. Then Tricia and I could hang out all the time. As soon as I have that thought, I cheer up right away.

"I'll help you with the groceries," I tell Tricia quickly. "But this building will be really cool. Manuel is already talking about what kind of trucks he'll see at the construction site. And Mrs. Lewis might move there, and her family really needs a new apartment. They live in a one-bedroom, and they're in Pine Hill all the time for ballet anyway—it would be so much easier living in the new building than driving from East Bolton every day."

Jayden clears his throat. "I don't know who Mrs. Lewis is, but I need a place for my wheels."

I want to roll my eyes. Jayden only got into skateboarding, like, this year. It's not *that* important.

Tricia straightens up and folds her hands. "Sofía, it's really cute that you're worried about Mrs. Lewis. But it's not nice for anyone if there's a big ugly building right there."

I really don't get what Tricia is saying. The way my mom described the building, it's going to be gorgeous. I remember how my parents always talk about living in Cuba with *their* parents and not knowing if they would ever be able to have their own apartment, let alone a house. So I start to tell Tricia that.

"You know," I say, "sometimes it's *really* hard for people

to find new apartments if they don't build enough of them. When my parents were in Cuba—"

Tricia cuts me off. "You're always talking about Cuba."

Do I really talk about Cuba that much? I mean, compared to my family, I barely ever mention Cuba.

"My grandparents were Cuban," Tricia goes on, "Stella's are Italian—"

"Well, but I don't mind—" Stella starts to say, but Tricia interrupts her.

"You don't see the rest of us carrying on about where our families are from all the time."

I swallow hard and try to look straight ahead, not focusing on anything, but I can still see Tricia and Stella. Tricia is sitting up very straight, and Stella's eyes look like they're going to pop out of her head. I don't remember Tricia ever being this nasty to me—usually, she sticks up for me against my sister or Mrs. Jansen or people like Jayden. I don't know why this is different. It's just an apartment building.

I pick up my fork and shove a piece of crinkly green something or other in my mouth. Turns out fancy lettuce is grosser than regular lettuce.

When dessert comes out, I'm hungry enough to have six of the cookies they bring, but even those are kind of boring. I think they forgot the sugar. I'm about to make a joke about how they must have known a Cuban was coming, but then I remember what Tricia said and keep my mouth shut. A lady who works at the country club gives a little speech about how proud she is of the students in Modern Manners, because they learned how to be considerate and respectful at the table. I pretend to listen.

When the party's over, Tricia and I head outside to wait for her mom to pick us up. As soon as we get there, I turn to Tricia.

"Why are you being so mean?"

Tricia shakes her head. "You always try to force this Cuban stuff on me."

"I do not! I always want to *talk* to you about it. About what it's like for you, being Latina and—"

"But I'm not," Tricia says. "I don't feel Latina like you. I don't speak Spanish, my dad never talks about it, and it doesn't matter to me."

"You don't have to speak Spanish to be Latina!" Lots of Latinas don't speak Spanish. I don't mean to make Tricia feel bad that she doesn't—I just wish she would be nicer to people who do.

"It's not just Spanish," Tricia goes on. "It's all the other stuff. I wish you would just *shut up* about it."

"Fine." I zip my lips. I decide not to say anything else about Cuba or Yolanda or Álvaro to Tricia, if that's what she wants. But I don't know what else to say to her, either.

Mrs. Rivera doesn't seem to realize anything has happened with Tricia and me, because she gives me a big hug and asks us about the party. I let Tricia answer. As we're heading toward her car, Mrs. Rivera stops me.

"Sofía!" she exclaims. "Look at your skirt!"

I look down at my hem, which is still sort of crooked.

"Did you do that yourself, darling?"

"I wanted to decorate my dress a little bit. You know, for the party."

Mrs. Rivera laughs and shakes her head. "You are a cute kid, Sofía Acosta. A cute, funny kid. Did anyone ever tell you that?"

I shrug. Mrs. Rivera laughs even louder. "I don't know how your mom keeps up with you," she says, climbing into the driver's seat.

I sit very primly during the ride home. I think about Tricia, and about what the lady said about Modern Manners teaching respect and consideration for others. I didn't go to Modern Manners, but I'm getting the feeling that you really learn the opposite of what the lady said. It's like my best friend went to special classes to learn how to be mean to me.

It's a good thing we can't afford the country club, because I don't think I would ever want to be a member anyway.

CHAPTER TWENTY-FOUR

It's our first dress rehearsal at the Pine Hill Playhouse, otherwise known as my favorite day of the year. It's a frosty Monday afternoon in December, and by four o'clock it's nearly night out. The theater is old and drafty, and I have my fuzzy purple hoodie on over my white leotard and tights so I can stay warm until it's time to get into our costumes. When we get to the theater, I race down the center aisle. I remember how Tricia and I strolled around last year, past the gilded walls and silhouettes, imagining we were elegant Victorian ladies. We were only angels then, but we were already dreaming of being in Party Scene. Now it's finally here, but I don't even know where Tricia is. At school today she answered all my questions with "Yes" or "No" and barely said anything the whole day. A part of me thinks I should be mad at *Tricia*, not the other way around, but another part of me is nervous and just wants to make up with her.

Our dressing room is backstage on the second floor. Party

Scene kids are in a separate dressing room from the younger kids, while Regina and the other teenagers are down on the first floor backstage. The second floor is total mayhem. My mom and Mrs. Lewis are shouting themselves hoarse trying to get kids to line up for their costumes, which have all been altered and steamed by Mrs. Lewis. She's pinned a big label to each costume with the right person's name on it, but that doesn't stop some of the younger kids from reaching up and grabbing one without looking.

Two kindergarteners run by dressed as mice, and I wish Tricia were there to *aww* with me. We were mice together in kindergarten too, and we've been friends ever since. But now Tricia is over in the corner talking to Stella. I line up to get my costume, keeping one eye on them.

They're heading this way, and Stella waves at me.

"Hi, Sofía!" she says brightly. I think she's trying to make up for how awkward the Modern Manners party was.

"Hi," I say, and Tricia lifts one hand, giving me a short wave. We stand silently on line. When my turn comes, I reach for my dress and slip it on over my head. As soon as I do, a shiver runs up my spine. I don't feel like Sofía anymore. I feel like a Victorian girl. I imagine I live in Germany a hundred years ago, in a big house where gingerbread is baking in the oven. I'm going to a party at my friend Clara's house tonight, where a mysterious man will bring a nutcracker doll and cast a spell bringing all the toys and mice to life. I can't help myself. I turn to Tricia.

"Do you feel it?" I whisper.

She smiles a tiny bit, then nods. "I feel it," she says. "It's *Nutcracker* time."

I spread my hands over my silky skirt, beautifully trimmed with ribbons and bows I sewed myself, not the least bit crooked. I did it. We did it. Here I am, about to be in Party Scene.

We're all headed to the stage when Mrs. Lewis stops us. "Party Scene kids!" she shouts. "Hold up!" She digs her phone out of her pocket and motions for us all to get together. I grin while she takes the photo. I'll finally have a picture of me and all my friends in Party Scene to hang on my side of the bedroom.

Mrs. Lewis puts her phone away. "Off you go now! Don't be late!" She looks up and smiles at me, then pulls me into a one-armed hug. "The costumes look great, Sofía."

My mom meets my dad and me in the wings just as the overture comes crackling over the theater's audio system. I can't believe how much bigger and fuller it sounds here after weeks of only hearing it on phones and the speakers at Mrs. Jansen's. Some performances of *The Nutcracker* have a live orchestra and everything. We're not nearly fancy enough for that, but just hearing it on the big loudspeakers, coming from all directions, is enough for me. I bounce up and down excitedly. My parents are also dressed as Victorians, which is pretty funny. There are a bunch of other grown-ups playing parents in Party Scene, but I'm the only kid who has my *own* parents playing my parents in the show, too. It's really fun, and when it's our turn to skip onto the stage as if we're just arriving at the party, I don't feel like Sofía, the middle Acosta child who isn't actually that good at ballet. I feel like Party Scene Girl #3, happy to be going to my friend's Christmas party with my family. I think we need a new German-Victorian-y-sounding name, so I make one up: we'll be the Hoffmanns. The man who wrote the original *Nutcracker* story was called E. T. A. Hoffmann, so I think it's a fitting last name. I turn around to tell my parents, but I don't realize that at that exact moment we're supposed to be pretending to receive delicious candy, so instead of talking to my mom, I find myself talking to the velvety fabric of the wings.

"CUT!" The music stops, and Mrs. Jansen stomps her black boots. "Sofía Acosta, you just missed your cue! Look where everyone else is standing!"

I turn back toward the stage, and sure enough, everyone is somehow clumped up by the fake Christmas tree, eating their fake candy. I have no idea how I ended up in the wrong place. I just wanted to tell my parents about my great new German name.

"Sorry, Mrs. Jansen," I squeak. My mom takes me by the elbow and gently leads me over to the right place.

Mrs. Jansen makes the whole cast go back to the beginning of Party Scene. While the overture is playing again, I explain to my parents.

"I was just thinking that we should have a German last name while we're in the show, because, you know, Acosta doesn't really sound like a family who would be invited—"

"*Shhhh!*" My mom gives me a stern look and puts her finger to her lips. My dad raises his eyebrows as if to say, "Aren't you listening?"

This time things go a little better. I remember to run over to the Christmas tree with everyone else to have imaginary candy. But then, during the March, I'm so focused on bringing my feet *down* on the downbeat, the way my dad and Regina always insist, that I accidentally bring my foot *down* on Greg. Hard. *Really* hard. I was trying to dance with emphasis!

Greg yelps and grabs his foot.

"STOP!" Mrs. Jansen yells. Whoever is running the audio system doesn't hear her, and she waves her hands toward the back of the theater. Everyone is frozen in place until the music finally stops.

Now Mrs. Jansen's face is red, and her eyebrows are knit tightly together. "Sofía Acosta, let me ask you a question."

I gulp.

"Have you had your eyes checked recently?"

"Ummm. Yes?"

"So if there is no problem with your eyesight, you should be able to see your friend's feet, don't you think?"

"Yeah."

"Are you going to apologize to Greg?"

"Sorry," I squeak. Greg shrugs. He doesn't seem hurt, really.

Mrs. Jansen buries her face in her hands. Then she grabs me and Greg each by the shoulder and moves us toward the back of the stage. She has Stella and her partner slide over so they're closer to the front, even though Stella is taller and usually tall people go farther back. "Let's try this. We can't have you so close to the front if you can't follow the music."

My face burns, and I look back at my parents, who are standing with the other grown-ups, milling around the fake Christmas tree. Their faces are blank, like they didn't even hear what just happened. I squeeze my eyes shut and blink very hard.

Mrs. Jansen presses a button on her watch. "There's no time to do a complete run-through now. We'll have to pick up where we left off." She waves her hands toward the back of the theater, and the music picks up again.

I can tell Greg feels bad. "It wasn't such a big deal," he mumbles while we make our way through the rest of the motions. "I was just surprised. Shoulda kept my mouth shut."

I shake my head. "It was my fault. I'm just clumsy."

"No you're not," he says, even though I know it's true. Somehow Greg being so nice to me makes that feeling like I can't breathe and my chest is squeezing tight worse. I sneak a peek over my shoulder at my mom, and now I'm thinking about how some parents volunteer and some parents pay a fee. Greg's dad comes every year to hang the sets, and I never really thought about why he did that until right now. I have a huge lump in my throat, and by the time we line up for the Grandfather Dance, blurry tears are threatening to spill out. I blink them back and try to focus on the steps.

All the practice must have paid off, because I can do the Grandfather Dance okay even through tears. But then we get to the hop-step and I have to go backward and suddenly I'm all mixed up and I can't blink anymore, there are just puddles of tears spilling down, and when I reach up to wipe my eyes, I accidentally elbow Stella in the face. She pretends nothing happened and keeps dancing with a big smile on her face, but that just makes me cry harder. I fumble and start the next jump a half beat too late, landing on the far side of the stage, closer to where the parents are dancing.

I hear the words before Mrs. Jansen says them. "CUT! STOP!"

I don't even try not to cry anymore. People step back as if I'm diseased, and suddenly I'm in the middle of the stage, all by myself, crying my heart out. Manuel is standing with Dahlia, and there's an odd expression on his face. It's like he's so embarrassed to be related to me.

"Sofía," Mrs. Jansen says. "Honey. Can someone get her a tissue?" she snaps, and a mom runs out from the wing and hands me a paper towel. I blow my nose on it, even though it's hard and rough.

Mrs. Jansen shakes her head. "Sofía. We've tried. But this isn't working. Do you think it's working?"

I just keep crying.

"Sofía. Do you think this is working?"

"No," I whisper finally.

CHAPTER TWENTY-FIVE

I'm dressed in regular clothes, and my jeans feel heavy and stiff as I'm surrounded by people in silky tights and swishy costumes. It's opening night, and instead of being upstairs with Tricia and the other Party Scene kids, I'm sitting on a stool in Regina's private dressing room, which is on the ground floor closest to the stage. Mrs. Jansen let Zaria take my part in Party Scene, even though she had been cast in Hoops because she was too tall for Party Scene. Mrs. Lewis just let out one of the dresses so that it fit her, and now she's dancing both parts.

Regina is sitting in front of the mirror, fussing while my mom dusts her with blush.

"Ma, not too much—I don't want to look tacky!"

"Pero ¿cómo te vas a ver en el video?" My mom steps back, still holding the brush in one hand. There's a special videographer out in the audience that my parents hired to record Regina. His assistant is in the wings so they can shoot Regina's performance from multiple angles. My mom wants to make sure the lights don't wash out Regina's facial features, and they're arguing about it.

My parents are already dressed for Party Scene. My mom is wearing a dress with an enormous hoopskirt, and my dad is wearing an old-fashioned velvet suit with a lacy cummerbund. Except they are going to play Zaria's parents instead of mine. I wonder if they'll tell Zaria about my great idea to call our fictional Party Scene family the Hoffmanns. Or if they'll just call themselves the Acostas plus Zaria.

Regina doesn't go on until the second act, but she already has her costume on below layers of leg warmers and wrap-around sweaters to keep her muscles from getting cold. She'll finish her hair and makeup, my mom will spray everything to make it stay put, and then she'll jump and stretch around this dressing room to stay warm.

Regina and my mom argue about makeup some more, and after a few extra puffs of blush, my mom says "Ya" and puts down the brush. Telling Regina to close her eyes, she spritzes her with makeup-setting spray before switching to hairspray to make sure Regina has no flyaways or frizzes. Because Regina's hair is so curly, she needs a lot. I've always loved the way hairspray smells—a little fruity and a little tangy. Usually it smells exciting, like opening night. But right now the smell just bums me out.

"One more thing," my mom says.

"Ma," Regina groans. "I'm going to look like a painted clown."

But instead of reaching for more makeup, my mom takes something out of her shoulder bag.

The package is about the size of a lunch box and wrapped in many layers of tissue paper. I lean forward. It's not like my mom to wrap things; usually with gifts she asks me to wrap them for her or she just gives them to people unwrapped. But this package is tied up with a bow and everything.

"What's that?" Regina asks. She looks pale.

My mom smiles mischievously. "Una cosita. But first you have to read the card." She hands Regina a folded piece of pale pink stationery.

I peer over Regina's shoulder while she reads.

Querida Regina:

Cuando Alicia Alonso bailó su primer Giselle *con el Ballet Theatre en la Metropolitan Opera House de Nueva York, la bailarina Alicia Markova le dio la tiara que ella misma había llevado en *su* primer* Giselle. *Hoy continuamos la tradición, de Alicia a Alicia. Yo, tu mamá Carmen Alicia, te regalo a ti, Regina Alicia, la tiara que yo me puse en mi primer* Cascanueces, *hace muchos años en Cuba. No es tan elegante como las que se consiguen aquí en Estados Unidos, pero pensé que te daría fuerza y fe para tu show esta noche.*

Tu papá y yo estamos muy orgullosos de ti. Has trabajado mucho para llegar a este momento. Nunca esperamos tener una hija como tú, con tanta gracia y talento. Te queremos mucho, nuestra Dewdrop linda.

Mami y Papi

It means:

Dear Regina,

When Alicia Alonso danced her first Giselle *with Ballet Theatre at the Metropolitan Opera House in New York, the ballerina Alicia Markova gave her the tiara that she had worn in *her* first performance of* Giselle. *Today we continue the tradition, Alicia to Alicia. I, your mother Carmen Alicia, give you, Regina Alicia, the tiara that I wore when I danced my first lead in* The Nutcracker, *many years ago in Cuba. It's not so fancy as the ones they make here in the United States, but I thought it would give you strength and faith for your show tonight.*

Your father and I are very proud of you. You have worked very hard to get to this point. We never dreamed of having a daughter with so much talent and grace. We love you a lot, our pretty Dewdrop.

Mami and Papi

My eyes feel hot and prickly again, like they have time after time the last few days. Regina rips off the tissue paper, and inside is a glittering tiara, simple but elegant, with patterns of rhinestone flowers and touches of white lace on the sides. It was clearly made by hand. Fragile and precious. I've been tinkering with headpieces for Stella and Tricia's Decorations Committee, and I can tell the work of a master when I see one. I don't know who made that headpiece, but I could never make anything like it. My mom places it carefully on Regina's head and bobby-pins it in place. They look at themselves in the mirror, together, and my dad leans over my mom's shoulder: three Acosta dancers.

There's a knock on the door, and it's Alejandro and Teresa, our neighbors. Mami and Papi asked them to sit in the audience with me tonight, since I'm not in the show. Yolanda and Álvaro are coming too, but I guess they're back in their seats. Alejandro and Teresa smile brightly at me and wave our tickets.

"¿Lista?" Teresa asks, putting an arm around me.

"Yeah, I'm ready," I say, grabbing my coat off the dressing room table. I don't waste any time hurrying out the door to be in the audience with all the people who are not my family. I can't wait to get out of this stuffy cubicle of a dressing room.

CHAPTER TWENTY-SIX

The last time I sat in the audience of the Pine Hill Playhouse, it was for a performance of *Cinderella* by an acting troupe from New York City. I didn't know any of them. My family was sitting on either side of me. Now the overture to *The Nutcracker* starts, and I stare at the wrong side of the curtain. I should be in the wings right now, wearing my beautiful Party Scene dress, with my parents on either side of me. I wonder if they're thinking about me, sitting out here without them, or if they're relieved that I can't mess up the show anymore. I scrunch down into my seat, putting the toes of my sneakers on the seat in front of me. Yolanda raises an eyebrow, but she doesn't say anything. I guess Álvaro doesn't feel like making jokes with me today, because he's staring straight ahead.

I don't feel like watching everyone dance without me, so I pay attention to the other people in the audience. It's too dark to see them clearly, but I can make out their shapes. Yolanda is following Carrie, who plays Clara, closely. She moves her head side to side with the music, almost mimicking Carrie's dancing. Álvaro's chin bobs in time. A few rows ahead of us, on the other side of the aisle, there's a man bringing his leg up and down, up and down. I guess everyone but me can tell the difference between an upbeat and a downbeat. I study Yolanda again. She's totally not paying attention to what she looks like, and something about the joy on her face reminds me of playing softball with Laurita on Thanksgiving, how when she reached for the ball, she wasn't angry at the world anymore. When the Grandfather Dance begins, I close my eyes, trying to tune out *The Nutcracker.*

At intermission, Yolanda and Álvaro get up from their seats before I get a chance to talk to them. Teresa and Alejandro take me to the very front of the theater, by the ticket booth, where some of the volunteer parents are selling candy canes and Christmas cookies. Teresa buys me a whole plate of candy and cookies. I know she's trying to cheer me up, but the cookies taste like nothing, and Teresa and Alejandro's bright conversation just makes me want to cry.

"Can I go outside for a second?"

Teresa bites her lip.

"I see some of my friends," I lie, motioning to the sidewalk through the glass doors, where lots of people are milling around.

"Come right back in," Teresa says. "Just a few minutes."

I nod and push open the glass doors. Outside, I take a deep breath of cold air. It's dark out, but the stores on Main Street have already hung their twinkle lights, and the lampposts are ringed with garlands. There are lots of kids from my school outside the playhouse, holding flowers to give to their friends after the show and talking about who danced really well, but I push past them, trying to find a quiet spot. At the end of the block, I stop and lean against a brick wall. I don't want to cry, but I can't stop it, either.

Sniffling through my tears, I overhear a conversation around the corner from where I'm standing. It's getting louder and louder, and I realize that the people are speaking Spanish. Not that many people in Pine Hill speak Spanish, so I peek around to see who it is.

I pull back immediately. It's Yolanda and Álvaro, and by the looks of it, they're fighting again.

Their sharp words clear my head and stop me from crying long enough to lean back around. They don't notice me watching them, because they're so busy fighting. "You don't care what happens to me," Álvaro hisses. "You just don't want to be left alone. Egoísta."

"Is it so much to ask?" Yolanda's voice is choked by a sob. "For a mother to want her son nearby?"

"Pero, Mamá, si tú vienes—"

"Oh, don't be silly," Yolanda snaps. "I belong in Cuba. In my home. You're being—an imperialista!" she spits at him.

I gulp. The Cuban government calls people from the United States imperialistas. My mom says it to Regina and Manuel and me when she thinks we're being selfish or materialistic.

Álvaro steps back. "You're jealous, Ma. You're jealous that everyone else knows how to live a good life. Everyone but you." He has one dagger left, and he throws it. "I'm staying, with or without you. See if I care."

Yolanda chokes back a sob and takes off running, her purse held close to her side. Álvaro stands there for a long minute, then puts his hand in his pockets and walks away, head hanging.

It takes me a long time to realize that neither of them is coming back for the second act of *The Nutcracker,* and I stay there staring at the spot where they were standing until the bells chime for the end of intermission. I hurry back inside, ignoring Teresa and Alejandro, who tell me a million times that they were worried and to stay where they can see me next time and all that. I think they're so worried about me that they don't notice Yolanda's and Álvaro's empty seats.

"Are you excited to see your sister dance Dewdrop?" Teresa says as we settle back into our seats. "You must be so proud of her."

"Uh-huh," I say, nodding.

I tell myself I am proud of Regina, but when the first strains of the Waltz of the Flowers crackle over the speakers, I feel awful. Regina *bourrés* onto the stage with her arms held gracefully, tinkly and light on pointe, just like a Dewdrop should be. I barely notice how the beads on her costume, the ones I sewed myself, sparkle in the stage lights, because I'm crying again and it's hard to see. The music picks up and Regina's dancing becomes more athletic, but delicate and musical at the same time. People clap and gasp, proud that one of Pine Hill's own is dancing a part usually done by a professional. She's dancing it *well*, too. The people at ABT would be stupid not to pick her for the Summer Intensive once they see this performance. But I don't *want* Regina to become a famous ballerina and leave our house forever in two years.

The Flowers dance around Regina, waving pink garlands overhead while she twirls and leaps. As the music winds up, faster and more triumphant in these last bars, I can't stop the tears. Ballet was supposed to be something that brought my family together. Ballet is how my parents met. It's how they came to the United States, how they bought our house and had my family. I thought that being a ballet family meant we would always be the Acosta Accordion, a family of dancers in Pine Hill. But now ballet is tearing everyone apart. It's the reason Yolanda and Álvaro are fighting, the reason Yolanda is going to be all alone when she goes back to Cuba. It's the reason Regina is going to go away someday, too. And most of all, it's the reason I don't fit in, the reason I don't belong in my family or in Pine Hill or maybe anywhere at all—because I'm the only one in this whole theater who doesn't get music and beats and rhythm and probably the only kid in the history of Mrs. Jansen's to ever get kicked out of *The Nutcracker*.

Regina takes bow after bow, the Flowers clear the stage, and the soft strains of the Sugar Plum *pas de deux* begin. The dancer is a stranger, someone Mrs. Jansen hired from the city. I know enough to tell that she doesn't have Regina's grace or strength, but I'm barely paying attention. Teresa notices me crying and puts an arm around me.

"Ya, ya," she whispers, stroking my hair. I'm so embarrassed I could run out of this theater right now. She holds me tight the rest of the show, and when the curtain closes and the lights come back on, she hands me a tissue and dabs my face, cleaning me up so that I can smile and talk to all the people rushing up to me to say how amazing Regina was.

It's forever before my family comes out from backstage. The theater has totally emptied out, and Teresa and Alejandro and I are the only ones left in the audience. The seats are the kind that fold up and down, so I'm entertaining myself by balancing on the top of the folded part, then plopping down when the seat opens. Teresa doesn't even tell me to stop.

Mrs. Jansen comes out and waves goodbye to me, hurrying past us like I might bite. I swallow hard. I wonder what can be taking my family so long, but finally they come out. My dad has his hands in his pockets, and my mom is talking on her cell phone. Regina is holding Manuel by the shoulders.

I meant to say something nice and sisterly about how Regina is a star now, but instead I take one look at them and blurt out:

"What happened?"

My dad takes his hands out of his pockets. He clears his throat. "Sofía, Yolanda and Álvaro . . ."

I realize my mom is talking to Yolanda on the phone.

"What is it?"

"Yolanda and Álvaro had a fight," Regina interrupts. "Álvaro got mad and went to stay with a friend in the city. He's not sleeping at our house anymore."

"Oh." I frown. "Maybe he'll come back soon! He has to see Yolanda at the ABT performance anyway."

"It's no fun being alone in my room," Manuel pipes up. "At least you and Regina have each other."

"You can stay in our room tonight," I promise Manuel as my dad pulls the car keys out of his pocket.

"Carmen," my dad says to my mom, who is still talking, "I'll take the kids home, okay?"

"We'll stay and give Carmen a ride," Teresa says immediately, and my dad kisses her and Alejandro gratefully.

My dad, Manuel, Regina, and I go silently to the car. My dad starts the engine, and Manuel bursts out, "This is no fair. I didn't even get to say goodbye to Álvaro!"

My dad smiles at us in the rearview mirror. "Actually, Manuel, you might be seeing *a lot* more of Álvaro after his ABT performance next week." He takes a deep breath. "Lo que tienen que entender is that Yolanda and Álvaro were fighting because next week when the rest of the Ballet Nacional de Cuba dancers go back home, Álvaro . . ." My dad hesitates.

"It's okay, Papi," I say. "I already know. Álvaro is going to stay in New York and join American Ballet Theatre."

Regina gasps. "Is that true? How did you find out?"

"Álvaro told me. I know we have to keep it a secret."

"Manuel, do you understand that?" my dad asks in a stern voice. "You can't tell anyone."

"Wait, so he *is* going to be my roommate again?" Manuel's fist pumps the air.

My dad laughs. "Just until he can get his own place."

The thought of Álvaro being our neighbor pushes out some of the sadness. I wish they would hurry up and build Acorn Corners right away.

Without thinking, I've been rolling my program up in my hands. I don't even notice until Regina shrieks.

"I need that to send in with my video! You're getting it wrinkled."

I roll my eyes, but I stop playing with the program and stare out the window. Ballet was supposed to be this thing that brought people together. Like my family performing in

The Nutcracker together. Like Regina saying that ballet crosses boundaries.

Except tonight, I had to watch *The Nutcracker* alone instead of being with my family, because I'm not good enough at ballet. Álvaro and Yolanda are fighting because ballet is pulling them apart, tearing them between two countries. Nothing has really changed since Alicia Alonso had to choose between Cuba and the United States.

Regina snatches the program from me and starts smoothing it out on her lap. I lean back in my seat. She can have it. I've had enough ballet-related fights tonight to last me a lifetime.

CHAPTER TWENTY-SEVEN

Even though *The Nutcracker* is over, there are still regular ballet classes at Mrs. Jansen's until Christmas break. When I show up for class the Wednesday after *The Nutcracker,* Mrs. Jansen's Ballet Academy feels different. Outside, everything seems the same: the cement stoop has cracks in all the same places and the UPS and FedEx boxes are topped with a light coating of snow. Inside, everything smells the same: the scents of steam and hairspray and sweaty feet mingle together in the exact same way. But it's like I'm seeing our ballet school through a blurry pair of glasses. I've been coming to Mrs. Jansen's for as long as I can remember, since I was a toddler. But now that I know I can be kicked out, I don't know how to think about this place anymore. I don't know if I should even be here at all.

Mrs. Jansen acts normal, as if nothing ever happened. She greets all the kids in my level and lines us up at the barre in the big studio. The whole class, I try to just focus on doing the steps right and staying away from everyone. I don't want to hear what a fun time other people had, or how many flowers they got after the show, or which pictures their parents are putting in the Christmas card. Mrs. Jansen doesn't say anything to me, nothing like "Sorry I kicked you out of *The Nutcracker* and ruined everything." She just keeps teaching ballet steps.

I purposely hang back after class, trying to be the last one out. I don't want to bump into anybody in the dressing room. But while I'm sitting on the floor of the big studio, pulling off my sweaty slippers, someone clears her throat. It's Tricia. She's standing above me, holding something in her hand.

I stand up, not really knowing what to say. Before I can think of anything, Tricia throws her arms around me. "I'm sorry you didn't get to be in Party Scene with us. And I'm sorry I was mean to you at the Modern Manners party. I was just nervous because you know how I like Jayden—"

I didn't know that, actually—I didn't even know we were old enough to have people we liked now—but I hug Tricia back all the same.

"I can't believe I missed being in Party Scene with you."

Tricia pulls out of our hug and wipes her eyes. "That's the thing. I brought you this picture, the one of all of us at the dress rehearsal." She holds it out to me, and I take it. Everyone in the photo is smiling, all dressed up, with curled hair and makeup. "It doesn't matter that you weren't in the show," Tricia goes on. "That's just dancing. But those dresses! They were really special."

"Thanks, Tricia," I say softly, still holding on to the photo. I finally have what I wanted—a photo of me and my friends as Party Scene kids. I can hang it on my side of the bedroom, just like Regina has hers. But mine will always make me a little sad.

As we walk out of the studio, Tricia changes the subject to school, and I'm glad we don't have to keep talking about *The Nutcracker*. In the hallway, I see Mrs. Lewis, who gives me a high five. "How's my little seamstress doing? Are you going to help me for the next show, too?"

I glance at the door, where Mrs. Jansen is locking up. I can't tell if she heard. "Yeah, maybe," I say, noncommittal. Mrs. Lewis follows my gaze toward Mrs. Jansen, then suddenly pulls me into a big hug. I squeeze her back. I don't know how to say thank you to Mrs. Lewis. Guilt gnaws at my insides, the way it does when I think about my mom struggling in Cuba, and everything she does for us here. I think about Mrs. Lewis sharing a tiny apartment with Mike and Jessie and I wish Acorn Corners would get built right *now* and not next fall. I don't understand why I can never help the people I love, no matter how much I want to.

Mrs. Rivera is talking on her cell phone when we get out to the front. "I'll be done soon; this is just an important call," she says to Tricia, cupping her hand over the phone. She ducks inside to keep talking, and Tricia and I wait on the stoop for her. My mom is late anyway.

It's not that cold for December, and it's hard to believe

that *The Nutcracker* is already over. Next week is Álvaro's big performance at the Met, then it's Mr. Fallon's party, and right after that is Christmas. It should probably be snowing or something, but actually it's just kind of gray out. Tricia digs into her ballet bag and pulls out the hand towel her mom always puts in there so that she can wipe off her sweat before getting dressed. She reaches out and wipes off the top of the UPS and FedEx drop boxes, which are covered in a slight layer of frostiness. Then she slides onto the UPS box and waves her hand for me. I sit down next to her on top of the FedEx box. We smile at each other. It feels *right,* sitting on these boxes with Tricia. Stella has gone home already, and it's like it used to be, back when it was just Tricia and me in Level 5: two best friends.

We swing our legs over the edge of our UPS and FedEx boxes, letting our heels hit the metal, making hollow clanging sounds.

"So . . . ," I say slowly. "You really *like* Jayden?" It still seems weird to me. Jayden is just another goofball in our class.

"It's awful," Tricia goes on. "I feel so awkward around him, and I'm so nervous when we talk, like there are butterflies in my stomach."

A crush always sounded like a nice thing to me, but now that Tricia talks about hers, it doesn't sound fun at all.

"At least you have that boy living with you," Tricia says. "You know how to act around them."

"Álvaro?" I laugh. "He's like another brother. And anyway, he moved out."

"He did?"

I don't know why Tricia is suddenly interested in Álvaro. She never seemed to care about him before. But I guess now that his big performance at the Met is getting closer and she's into boys, Álvaro is cool.

"Yeah, he did." I finger the strap of my ballet bag. "I have a secret too, actually."

"You can tell me," Tricia says softly. "I told you my secret."

Suddenly I'm dying to tell Tricia about Álvaro. She just poured her heart out to me, after all. And Álvaro is someone from Cuba who Tricia actually seems interested in. I guess she doesn't mind my talking about Cuba if it involves handsome teenagers and American Ballet Theatre. So I lean in close, and with our heads together, I tell Tricia about how Álvaro will be joining ABT, even though people will say he's a defector and his mom will be hurt and miss him all the time.

Tricia listens closely, but when I'm done, she pulls her head away. "So he's going to break *the law*?"

I hadn't really thought of it that way. "The laws aren't really fair," I explain. "Álvaro is an amazing ballet dancer—why shouldn't he join ABT?"

"B-but—" Tricia sputters, and she sounds as surprised as I was to learn that she has a crush. "Immigrants shouldn't just sneak into our country. That's a big problem."

"Sneak into the country? What are you talking about? He has an invitation to join *American Ballet Theatre*—that's like the most important ballet company in *the world*." I don't know why Tricia isn't getting this. "He isn't being sneaky. He'll be dancing on a stage with hundreds of people in the audience." I almost say "Duh," but I keep it in.

Tricia crosses her arms. "Yeah, why do you think it's so hard for Americans to get into American Ballet Theatre? There are only so many spots and they keep giving them to people who shouldn't even be here anyway."

"Well—" I want to say that, first of all, America includes North and South America and the Caribbean, so technically Cuba *is* in America, but I know what Tricia means. She thinks only people born in the United States should get into American Ballet Theatre. "Anyone who's good enough can get into ABT," I say. "Look at Regina. She's definitely going to get in."

Tricia flips her hair over her shoulder. "Because they care about diversity."

The way she says *diversity* makes it sound like some kind of illness.

"No, because she's the best ballerina her age!"

Tricia glares at me, and I glare back.

"Fine," she says finally. "Regina is good. I bet Álvaro is good too. But I still think that people from here should have the first shot at a job at ABT. It's not fair that Álvaro is going to take a job from someone else. Besides, if we keep having so many immigrants in this country, there'll be no room left for the rest of us!"

It is pretty strange to hear an only child who lives in a huge house and has a bedroom and a playroom all to herself complain about having enough room. I grasp at air, trying to find a way to make Tricia get it.

"Weren't *your grandparents* immigrants, Tricia?" I promised not to bring it up to her. But I can't help it.

Tricia rolls her eyes. "That was different, Sofía. It was a long time ago and they weren't sneaking around like some immigrants."

The way she says *sneaking around* makes me want to scream. I wonder if Tricia knows any of the things I've learned from Laurita—about how hard the rules make things.

"Álvaro needs this job," I say. "Just as much as anyone in New York does. It's hard for him in Cuba, and he's not happy with the roles he's able to dance there. He wants to try out life in New York. I think he deserves a shot. And once you see him dance—" I shrug. "You should come to his performance. Once you've seen him in action, you'll be glad he's moving to the United States." I make sure to say the United States and not America.

"It's not our problem why he needs this job. It's our problem to make sure he's not taking a role away from an American who deserves it."

She's using an imitation grown-up voice and it makes me

mad. I guess now that Tricia has a crush, she thinks she's an adult all of a sudden. I throw my hands up and am about to reply, but at that moment Mrs. Rivera comes out to the stoop.

"All done, girls," she says cheerfully. "Ready to go, Tricia?"

CHAPTER TWENTY-EIGHT

It turns out the reason my mom was late picking me up is that she was comforting Yolanda, who is really upset about Álvaro having left. When we get to our house, I see that Laurita is waiting for me on the steps. I slap my hand to my forehead. "We're supposed to work on the exhibit tonight! I forgot."

My mom lets me jump out before she pulls the car into the driveway around back. I climb the steps and sit down next to Laurita. I wonder if we can work on our exhibit at her house, since Regina is probably inside watching her video for the ABT Summer Intensive for the zillionth time.

Laurita taps her notebook. "Did you get any information about Acorn Corners yet?"

"Ummm . . . I'm working on it," I lie.

"Okay," Laurita says, flipping open the notebook. "And I made the posters for all the stages of immigration."

So much for using puff paint, I think, but I don't tell Laurita that. It's my fault for not doing more work on this party.

Lately I keep messing everything up. I flip up the earflaps on my hat.

"Are you upset about something?"

"Are you kidding? You haven't heard that I got kicked out of *The Nutcracker*?"

"And?"

I sit up straight and tug down my earflaps. "It's *The Nutcracker*! And I'm an Acosta! It's like the most embarrassing possible thing that could happen to me. We're supposed to be good at ballet in this family, but I'm a mess. *Stella* is better at ballet than me now, and she's only been in my level for a few months!"

Laurita shrugs. "I got cut from the travel team I wanted last year. But I got in this year. Maybe you could be in *The Nutcracker* next year."

"Doubtful."

I'll never live this down. Ten years from now, I'll probably be carting Regina's suitcase around every hotel and theater on the planet while she's a famous ballerina. People will give me pitying looks and shake their heads. They'll wonder how someone with Acosta blood could have messed up so badly. Then they'll pat my parents on the shoulder and comfort them by telling them they got two out of three. There's a bad apple in every bunch, and that's me.

"You're making a really funny face. Like you're focusing hard on a test."

"I'm thinking about what's going to happen to me when I grow up," I growl, "and it's not pretty."

Laurita giggles. "You're not going to be grown up for a long time. I'm serious, you looked constipated." She giggles again.

I turn on her. "I can complain about whatever I want! *You're* the one who's always telling everyone bad news about recycling and country clubs and immigration and how your abuela is going to die!"

I suck in a breath sharply. I went too far, and I know it. Laurita looks like I slapped her. She purses her lips.

"Well, actually, I'm *not* trying to tell people bad news, if that's what you think. I'm *trying* to tell people to do something. I *hate* being a kid," she says savagely. "You can't do anything. Grown-ups can vote and drive and spend money, and instead of making it easier for other people, they just mess everything up and make it worse."

I cross my arms and lean over my knees. "It doesn't help when you say all this sad stuff. It just makes me feel bad. You're like my mom. She's always telling me about our friends in Cuba and how much they miss their kids in the United States when they can't get visas to visit. It's not like I can do anything about it anyway."

Laurita shakes her head. "Yes, you could do something about it. If you wanted grown-ups to know about how hard it is for your family—and mine, too—when we're worried about the people we love, you would be helping me with the exhibit. Look at all these powerful people in Pine Hill. Maybe if some of them learned something about immigration, they would act different." Laurita slaps her hand on the top of her notebook. "It's not much, but the exhibit is a chance to teach people. I'm not wasting it."

Across the street, the door to Laurita's house opens, and Mrs. Sánchez comes out flapping a dish towel. "¡Laurita!" she shouts. "¡Ven a ayudarme!"

Laurita stands and looks back at me awkwardly. "Look," she says. "I feel guilty too. I get it. That's the thing about when your parents are immigrants. The two of us got to grow up in this really nice place, but we know our parents didn't have it so easy."

She can say that again. I would give up everything my parents tell us to be grateful for—our house, our food, our school—if I could go back in time and give it to my mom and dad as kids instead.

Laurita goes on. "Every time my mom reminds me of what it was like for her in the Dominican Republic, I wish I could help her, and it makes me so angry when I can't. It's like . . ." Laurita searches for words. "Like I just want to rip someone to pieces because my mom had a hard life as a kid, and there's nothing I can do."

I sure know what she's talking about. My parents do everything for me, and I can't even give them one little hop-step in exchange.

"When I grow up," Laurita says, "I'm going to try to make sure what happened to my mom doesn't happen to other immigrants. Maybe then it will be fair."

I go inside and find my mom sitting at the kitchen table, drinking café con leche with Yolanda, whose face is streaked with tears. I pause. I wish there were something I could say to make Yolanda feel better. I wish I could say she could visit Álvaro anytime she wanted. But I know it might be a long, long time before Yolanda can get a visa from the United States again. It stinks. I wish everyone could just live wherever they wanted and visit as often as they wanted, and in my heart, I know that Tricia is wrong. What she said is wrong. It's hard enough for Álvaro to decide to stay in the United States, for Yolanda to be left behind, to need visas and permissions and have to go through hassles and spend lots of money just to see each other for a visit. No one in Pine Hill should make that any harder for them.

Upstairs, Regina is on my dad's tablet, watching her performance of Dewdrop again and again, chewing her nails nervously.

"You're going to get in," I say grumpily, and Regina shakes her head, like even my saying that could jinx it.

I throw myself on the bed. I'm proud of Regina, I think.

But I'm more proud of my mom, who is trying to help her friend.

CHAPTER TWENTY-NINE

The journal prompt for Mr. Fallon's class is *If I were president* . . . and I know just what to write about. I write that if I were president, I would make sure that everyone had a good place to live. They would live with their families, and they would be near whatever activities they needed to get to. I peek at Tricia, sitting next to me, and I add that maybe everyone could also live near the grocery store so they wouldn't have to carry heavy bags a long way. Immigrants wouldn't have to be separated from their families, like Laurita's abuela, or from their best friends, like my mom and Yolanda. I have so many ideas that I'm startled when Mr. Fallon asks anyone if they would like to share. My hand shoots into the air.

When Mr. Fallon calls on me, I falter for a minute. I look at what I've written and frown. Some of it might remind Tricia of our conversation yesterday, and it's already been weird all morning today. We sit right next to each other, after all. But I take a deep breath and say that if I were president, immigrants would never have to be separated from their families.

"Why is that important to you, Sofía?" Mr. Fallon asks.

"Well," I say. "Because—" I notice Tricia is sharpening her pencil into her mini-sharpener, even though the container is totally full of shavings. The top is going to pop off if she doesn't stop soon.

"Sofía? Do you want to tell us why this topic is so important to you?" Mr. Fallon repeats.

I shake my arms a little bit and focus on Mr. Fallon. "Yeah. I guess—well, I guess it's because my family is from Cuba."

Jayden sniggers. I turn to make a face at him, but Laurita is already giving him such a withering scowl that Jayden stops laughing right away. I need to learn how Laurita does that.

It's like being on a big stage with the spotlight shining on you. I wonder if this is what Regina felt like when she danced Dewdrop. Except Regina was radiant as Dewdrop, and I just wish I could shrivel up and be standing somewhere else. Tricia puts down her pencil and meets my eyes. Her expression isn't exactly encouraging.

Then I look over my shoulder and see Laurita watching me carefully. I remember the day we first talked about country clubs—how mean people were and how surprised I was that Laurita had tears in her eyes, even though it would make anyone cry. I used to think that just because Laurita had all these opinions, she didn't care what people said, but now I wonder if everyone cares. Maybe everyone is hurt when their class-mates tease them or their friends disagree with them, even enough to cry. The difference is that some people just say their ideas anyway.

So I do. I tell Mr. Fallon and my classmates about my parents. I tell them that they couldn't find an apartment in Cuba, and how sometimes they even had trouble getting enough food. I tell them about how hard it is for our family and other Latinos we know—I don't mention Laurita because it's not my business—that you can't even see your friends and relatives sometimes, let alone help them get visas and come to the United States, no matter how bad you miss them. I even say how I sometimes wish I could go back in time and help my parents—and that if I were president, I would *do* something, because the only thing better than going back and helping my parents would be going forward and helping everyone else.

When I'm finished, I don't feel like shriveling up. My cheeks are burning, and I'm glad I'm not as light as Regina—no one can see the red when my cheeks get hot. I sit down quickly. No one responds, but when Mr. Fallon tells us to get our math books, Stella whispers to me, "That was really *good*, Sofía. You're such a great writer."

Which is funny, because I didn't even read my writing—I just said what I meant. But it gives me a kind of glowing feeling inside that Stella said that, even if Tricia is quiet the rest of the school day.

It's a party-planning day, which means that Mr. Fallon

is supposed to leave right after school. Mrs. Kalinack did all that work making sure he had appointments and wouldn't be hanging around the gym, where we're meeting. I'm about to head downstairs when Mr. Fallon asks me to stay behind.

I shift in my seat, wondering if I'm in trouble. But the room empties out, and Mr. Fallon smiles and straddles his stool, right across the desk from me. He doesn't seem mad.

"Sofía, you had a lot of great ideas during your journaling time today."

I nod, not sure where this is going.

"You know I'm an immigrant to the United States too? I became a citizen this summer."

I cough nervously. Maybe Mr. Fallon suspects we're working on a party and is trying to weasel it out of me. Maybe I'm, like, the worst secret-keeper in the fifth grade and that's why he picked me to stay behind.

"Your ideas meant a lot to me," Mr. Fallon says. "Like you really care about people like me."

"But you have it so much easier than other immigrants," I blurt out. "It's not like you had to cross the border, and everyone thinks it's just *great* when you become a United States citizen. People aren't like that when it's Latinos."

Mr. Fallon eyes me thoughtfully. "You're probably right," he says. "I'm a very lucky immigrant. I spend a lot of time thinking about that, you know. It makes me angry—I wish there were more I could do to help."

"Really?" I'm surprised, because Mr. Fallon is a grown-up

and, like, the most popular person in our entire school. But right now he sounds like Laurita and me, just frustrated about how we can't help our parents or our grandparents or Yolanda and Álvaro.

"Sometimes I want to tear my hair out."

Wow.

"But you know," Mr. Fallon goes on, "then I talk to students like you, and it gives me a lot of hope. I want you to share your ideas whenever you can, Sofía. They might make a difference to a lot of people."

My heart swells, and there's a happy, bubbling feeling in my stomach. I wonder if this is what Regina feels like when Mrs. Jansen talks to her about her ballet dancing.

Mr. Fallon pauses for a minute. "But, Sofía," he says, "I'm still curious why you seemed so sad all day, even after doing such great work."

Oh. I guess it was obvious, then. I want to tell Mr. Fallon about it, but I don't want to rat out any of my friends. So I shrug. "Not everyone agrees with me. Some people think I'm obsessed with being Cuban, and like—they think we should have an extra parking lot instead."

Mr. Fallon raises an eyebrow. I'm not making any sense. It's all muddled up in my brain. I try again.

"I mean, when I talk about wanting to make things better for people, I know that some people don't think they should be better. They don't think—" I try to put into words how

Tricia and Jayden reacted to the new apartment building, or how Tricia is always afraid to say anything whenever she's around Altagracia. "They get uncomfortable," I finish. And then I realize that I know a lot about what Tricia thinks, because she's my best friend. I know how she feels when she hears about new apartment buildings or when she meets new people at my house, which is always full of new people. "They don't want things to change. They like everything the way it is. They don't want to feel like they don't speak the right language and it's awkward to talk—so they would rather everything just stay exactly the way it is, even if it makes it harder for other people."

Mr. Fallon nods wisely. "I get it. I have a lot of friends like that."

"So what do you do?"

"I never know exactly what to do," Mr. Fallon says. "But I try to remember two things. One, that people's ideas change, so I should give them a chance—especially when those people are ten years old. Two, that not every friend and I share everything. I have friends who I talk to about being an immigrant, and friends who I talk to about my boyfriend, and friends who I talk to about soccer—and they're all different. That's okay."

"Like how I was one way when my family went to Cuba and I'm another way in Pine Hill."

"Exactly. But even if you don't share everything with every single friend—*no* friend should stop you from sharing your ideas, Sofía. People can disagree with you, but they can't stop you from speaking your mind."

Mr. Fallon gives me a fist bump, and he gets up from his stool. I guess our little chat is over. But when Mr. Fallon puts on his coat, I give him a big hug.

"I'll walk you to the front door," I say. "I want to make sure you get there without making any detours." I think my classmates and Mrs. Kalinack will thank me for this.

Mr. Fallon looks a little confused, but pleased all the same.

CHAPTER THIRTY

I run into the gym, ignoring Mrs. Kalinack, who says I'm late. No one has started working yet anyway. I'm beelining it to the basketball hoop, where Laurita is sitting in her usual spot. I don't even glance back at Tricia and Stella.

All of a sudden I'm bursting with ideas for our exhibit. Laurita probably doesn't even recognize me. I tell her I need the posters she made so I can fix them up. Laurita has a lot of great information that everyone should know, so I'm going to make sure her ideas shine with bright, illuminated posters. I'm going to make paper arrows to put on the gym floor with washi tape. They'll say things like DON'T FORGET TO READ THIS! and WAIT UNTIL YOU GET TO THE NEXT POSTER! and YOU WON'T WANT TO MISS THIS INTERESTING FACT! I think if Laurita always presented her ideas that way, people might not think of her as the Bad News Machine.

Of course I leave out that last part when I tell Laurita my ideas, and she scribbles them down with gusto. I can tell she's excited.

"And *then*," I go on, "we should have a section on challenges immigrants face—"

"—and how people can help them!" Laurita finishes. We high-five. There's a loud burst of laughter behind us, and we look over at the Decorations Committee. Lucas and Tricia are wrapping Abdul up with crepe paper like a mummy. Stella looks exasperated.

Laurita raises an eyebrow. "Good thing our exhibit will be beautiful."

"Yeah." I grin. Then I have a question. "So, Laurita, what *can* people do to help immigrants? It's, like, kind of hard, right?"

Laurita chews on her pencil eraser. Kind of gross, but okay. "I hate it when other kids act weird because they hear my mom speaking Spanish," she says finally.

"Me too!" I almost shout. "It's like, what's the big deal? Just say hello and be nice like you would to anyone else!"

Laurita writes that down.

"Grown-ups can vote," she goes on. "But kids can't really do that."

"But we can talk to adults," I say. "And tell them to vote to make things better for immigrant families."

"We should think of something specific for Mr. Fallon," Laurita says. "It's his party, after all."

"He *loves* it when we learn stuff about Irish culture," I say immediately. "He keeps talking about how he's going to bring us all corned beef on St. Patrick's Day, and I can tell it bugs him when Jayden and Lucas goof off and don't pay attention when he talks about Ireland."

"So maybe 'Listen and learn'?" Laurita says, writing it down.

"We should tie it back to Acorn Corners," I say nervously, because Laurita is probably going to remember that I haven't done any research. "Immigrants need places to live when they get here. So maybe something about making space?"

Laurita nods, and by the time Mrs. Kalinack dismisses us, our list of ideas is looking pretty good:

How Kids Can Help Immigrants

- Be friendly! Say hello, goodbye, and thank you like you would with anyone else. If you can learn how to say those things in a person's own language, they might be happy, but don't use their language in a teasing way—be nice!

- Tell grown-ups to vote for people who will make things better for immigrants.

- Listen and learn about immigrants' cultures.

- Be welcoming and make space for immigrants where you live.

"I'll turn this list into a poster," I tell Laurita. "It'll be my most gorgeous one yet."

CHAPTER THIRTY-ONE

Not exactly surprising, but Regina got into the Summer Intensive at American Ballet Theatre. Now she's not just gliding around the house, she's floating. She's dreaming of how often she'll see such and such principal dancer in the hallway, and today she found out that there's a picture of Alicia Alonso dancing *Giselle* in one of the studios and has vowed to curtsy in front of it every day she's there. I'm starting to think it might be a long summer. It's going to be weird having Regina go to a different camp than me (because let's face it, Regina and ABT might call it a Summer Intensive, but it's just summer camp for dance geniuses, right?). Every other summer we've both just taken ballet classes at Mrs. Jansen's until we go to Puerto Rico to visit my tía Aldema. But Regina won't be at Mrs. Jansen's this summer, and even though Tricia will be, I get the feeling she's going to be doing a lot of swimming and tennis playing at the country club without me.

So I'm down in the basement, thinking about how to

make summer more fun. I'm in my hiding spot, hand-sewing the headband I want to give Manuel for Christmas. He's at his ballet class, and Regina is shut in our room, talking to one of her friends about her marvelous summer plans, I'm sure. My parents are working late, so Altagracia is here, making dinner in the kitchen.

At dinner that evening, I look guiltily across the table at Yolanda. She has definitely been even more depressed since Regina got into the ABT Summer Intensive. It's the last week of Yolanda's trip, and I hate that she's miserable. Regina has tried to avoid talking about ABT around Yolanda, but she can't help saying how excited she is to hang out with Álvaro at 890 Broadway, which is where ABT rehearses in New York City. She can't wait until Álvaro's secret is out in the open so she can tell Bridgit and Cassadie all about it.

I set down my fork. I just realized something. *I told Tricia about Álvaro.*

I gulp down the rest of my dinner nervously. I wonder if Tricia will tell her mom. I had been doing such a great job keeping Álvaro's secret. If Tricia ruins it for him—I can't even think about it.

"¿Mañana vamos a esa reunión?" I hear my dad say.

I listen halfheartedly to the grown-ups' conversation. It's about some meeting they're going to at our town hall.

"Of course they would put it at three in the afternoon,

when almost no one who works can go," my mom complains in Spanish, shaking her head.

Yolanda says with a hollow laugh, "All this worry over a new building? In Cuba we would throw a party if they built a new apartment building in the neighborhood!"

"Here, too," my dad says. "It's just some people are so bigoted that a few new apartments and they complain."

I start to piece together what they're talking about. "Wait," I say. "They're having a meeting about Acorn Corners?"

Regina rolls her eyes. "Planet Earth calling Sofía! Where have you been? A bunch of moms in Pine Hill are complaining about the building."

"Oh yeah," I say. "I heard about that. But it will be great to have Mrs. Lewis living nearby, and—" I shut my mouth quickly. I almost said, "I think Álvaro could live there too," but I remembered just in time.

"Well, those moms are going to try to stop the construction," Regina says.

"What? That's not fair!"

Yolanda and my dad are still talking, and Yolanda asks what the big deal is.

"The people complaining say the apartments will ruin the small-town feel of the neighborhood," my dad says. "But really, they just don't want more Black and Latino families living here. It scares them."

It seems silly that anyone would be scared of having Mrs.

Lewis or Álvaro as new neighbors. But the more I think about what my dad is saying, the more the people trying to stop the construction make me feel a little sick.

My mom puts her hand on my back. "¿Quieres venir a la reunión?"

At first I think, Why would I want to go to a boring grown-ups' meeting?

But then my mom explains that people might want to hear from a kid like me. "All the moms are going to say that they don't want the new building because it will be worse for their kids. If they hear from a kid who *wants* the building, it might really make a difference."

I consider what my mom is saying. I imagine Jayden's mom coming to the meeting with his skateboard in her arms, cradling it and sobbing about how he'll have nowhere to ride now. Okay, so she probably wouldn't cradle Jayden's dirty skateboard and cry, and *anyway* Jayden can ride his skateboard in the park, but my mom has a point. If I could say, "Actually, kids don't really need that parking lot because we have an actual park, but we do really need new neighbors," that might help. I smile and nod at my mom. I'll come to the meeting with her. Then, of course, Yolanda says she'll come too, and I find out that Alejandro and Teresa decided they wanted to come also, so it looks like it will be a party.

* * *

Luckily, lunchtime at school the next day is one of our secret planning meetings for Mr. Fallon's party, so I don't have to talk to Tricia. We have a substitute too (I guess that's why Mrs. Kalinack thought it would be a good time to do party planning), which means we have a lot of silent work to do. I just keep my head down, and at lunch, I throw myself into the exhibit Laurita and I are designing. I'm working on a poster with information about famous immigrants. Laurita is a little better with the details and facts, but I help bring each poster to life so that the parents and the other kids who come to the party will actually want to read them and not think they're boring. While I'm working, I glance across the gym at Tricia a few times. She seems to be enjoying working on the decorations just fine, and I wonder why she hasn't complained about *Mr. Fallon* taking a job from someone else. My eyes narrow and I keep gluing beads to the border of my poster.

After school, I wait with Manuel on the school lawn until Regina walks over from the middle school to pick him up. Then I go straight to town hall to meet my parents, plus Yolanda, Alejandro, and Teresa. I love Pine Hill's town hall because it's like something out of a picture book. It has two stately white columns in the front, and a steep pointed roof. Inside, there's a room like an auditorium, but with folding chairs and a center aisle with plush red carpet like a king or queen would walk down, or a bride.

As my parents predicted, there aren't many people at the

meeting. My mom and dad were able to leave school in time to get here, but otherwise it's mostly empty. There's an older man in a wrinkled polo shirt standing at a podium near the front of the room. Mrs. Rivera is there with Stella's mom, and they both give me hugs and kiss my parents hello. Then my parents usher me into a seat, and our group takes up an entire row.

The meeting starts and I listen while the man in the polo shirt talks about the purpose of this meeting. Then a man in a nice suit, who showed up a little late, stands up and talks about why the building will be great. It turns out he works for the company that's making the building. He has a slide show with some pictures of what the apartments will look like, and I'm starting to think my parents should sell our house and move us to this building—none of the kitchens in the photos have crud stuck between pieces of linoleum floor. But afterward, when the man in the polo shirt opens things up for comments, I get confused. Someone raises their hand and says that the building is going to make it more expensive to live in Pine Hill, because there will be more kids going to school here, and that means everyone who already lives here might have to pay more money in taxes for school. I never knew I was so pricey, but suddenly I'm nervous. Regina already told me how my parents can barely afford our house and our food and our pointe shoes—will the new building make things even harder for them? At first it seems that I'm the only kid here.

Then I look over my shoulder and see Laurita! She's sitting in the last row, on the aisle, carrying a spiral notebook. She must have come in late.

But when my parents stand up to speak, I know that the building is a good idea. They tell everyone that we live right by where the new building will be built, and we welcome our new neighbors. I glow with pride that these are my parents.

Laurita raises her hand, and every single person turns around to face her. She looks so small, sitting there by herself. But she stands up, turns her notebook to a dog-eared page, and reads from her notes. She tells everyone that she supports the construction because it would help make Pine Hill more equal, fair, and diverse. My mouth hangs open just watching her talk. When did Laurita find time to prepare for this meeting, with softball, school, and planning our exhibit? Also, how is she so brave to talk in front of all these people?

A woman dressed in yoga clothing interrupts Laurita. She stands up and coughs, and suddenly it's like everyone forgot how interested they were in Laurita. Just because the woman is a grown-up, her voice carries more weight. Everyone turns their attention like it's a tennis match and the ball is in her court.

"All of us care about diversity and inclusion," the woman says in a commanding tone. "That's not the issue at hand. The issue here is the *character* of our community."

Mrs. Rivera rises from her seat and chimes in. "Exactly. We all moved to Pine Hill because we wanted to live in a small, tight-knit community where everyone knows everyone."

"More like a *rich* community where everyone knows everyone," Alejandro whispers to Teresa with a snort. Mrs. Rivera repeats again how much she cares about diversity. Then she suggests we start a fund for the Boys and Girls Club in East Bolton instead of making the new building. The woman in yoga pants volunteers to lead the fundraising effort.

"I know that recently there have been certain people who want to change our community," Mrs. Rivera is saying now, and she looks straight over at our row.

My eyes meet Mrs. Rivera's for a second, and then she looks away just as suddenly and faces the podium. It's like a bolt of lightning went up my spine, and I sit up straight, wriggling uneasily in my seat. What is Mrs. Rivera talking about? Why did she look at me? What "change" does she mean? Cold dread washes over me. Tricia *couldn't* have told her mom about Álvaro—she is always complaining to me about how strict her mom is.

But as Mrs. Rivera drones on, I get more and more nervous. Tricia complains about her mom's strictness, but she also follows her mom's rules. She talks to her mom a lot. I don't know why else Mrs. Rivera would be looking at me, except that Tricia told her about how Álvaro might move to Pine Hill. I don't think his moving here really counts as changing the community, but clearly Mrs. Rivera thinks it does. My heart beats faster and faster with every word she speaks.

"What everyone here has to understand," she finishes triumphantly, "is that we oppose this building because we care about our children and the place where they grow up. This is about THE KIDS."

My mom, my dad, Yolanda, Alejandro, and Teresa all look down the row at me. I know that's my cue to talk about how *I'm* a kid and I think the building would be great for me, but I can't talk. My throat is closing up. I feel my face getting hotter and hotter. I look desperately around the room, trying to find a way out. Laurita looks at me as if to say, "Well?" but I can't speak. Even if I had a fight with Tricia, I can't just disrespect a grown-up, and I'm scared that if I open my mouth, I'll blab about Álvaro to this whole room, just like I blabbed to Tricia. I can't trust myself. Maybe the new apartment building will make school more expensive. Maybe my parents and Laurita are wrong. Maybe, maybe, maybe. I lower my head, and the man in the wrinkled polo shirt calls on someone else.

CHAPTER THIRTY-TWO

The man in the polo shirt ends the meeting and says there will be another town hall after the holidays, and the vote on the construction will be then. It's like all this talk was for nothing. I watch while my mom and Mrs. Rivera kiss goodbye like nothing ever happened, as if my mom didn't hear Mrs. Rivera say what she said. Apparently my mom even knows the woman in the yoga pants, because they smile and chat with each other as we all shuffle out. When we reach the back, Laurita is still sitting in her folding chair. My mom swoops down and pulls her into an enormous hug.

"¡Mi cielo!" she exclaims. "You were amazing! Sofía, didn't she do great?"

I nod. "Yeah," I say weakly. "Awesome."

Laurita shrugs. "They didn't let me finish. I looked up some stuff about how the building could actually make taxes lower for everyone, because there would be more people to pitch in. But that lady cut me off."

"It didn't matter," my mom reassures Laurita. "You blew me away." She gives her another big squeeze. "¿Por qué no vienes a casa un ratico? Sofía hasn't had a playdate in ages."

Which is how I wind up at home with Laurita, playing catch with her and trying to think through what happened at the meeting at the same time. Amazingly, I still manage to catch most of the balls, but Laurita gives me a hard time about my throws.

"Are you even looking at me, Sofía?" She lobs the ball back hard, and I have to jump quick to catch it. I clutch the ball in my hands and stare at Laurita. Her tone was sharp.

The back door swings open and Manuel runs out with Eva and Jonah, all three of them sucking on lollipops. Manuel waves his at me.

"Regina bought us *candy* on the way home," he says. "How come you never do that?"

I throw the ball back to Laurita using all my strength. "Because I pick you up every day, Manuel. If I got you lollipops every day, I would have to be a millionaire."

Manuel sticks his strawberry-red tongue out at me while Eva zooms toward the big rock in the back of the yard.

"Are you all really going to climb that thing again?" I complain. "Mami and Papi don't like it."

"You're not in charge of us," Eva snaps at me, and I roll my eyes.

"Okay, Eva, you're right. You do whatever you want. See if I care."

Jonah, catching up to Eva, finds one of the footholds in the rock and tries to wriggle up. "Give me a push, Manuel," he calls.

Manuel looks back at me and bites his lip. He's torn, and I'm glad he's listening to me. But then Eva's voice pierces the air.

"Yeah, Emmanuel," she says, "let's climb to the top of the mountain today!"

Laurita drops the ball and whirls around. She marches up to Eva. Frizz pops free from her ponytail as she positions herself squarely in front of Eva.

Suddenly, Eva looks as small as she really is. "Let's get away from her," she says, backing up. "Come on, Emmanuel."

"Don't call him that," Laurita says bluntly.

Eva sticks her tongue out. "How come? Our teacher does it."

"Because it's rude, that's why. It's not his name and it's not what he asked you to call him. How about I start calling you Ester. That's kind of like Eva, isn't it?"

Eva doesn't seem to know what to say. I smile broadly. I think Eva might have finally met her match. Eva crosses her eyes at Laurita, then grabs Manuel by the hand.

"Let's go, Manuel."

Manuel links hands with Jonah, and the three of them run in a human chain to the other end of the yard. As they run, Manuel looks back over his shoulder and grins at Laurita, as if to say, "Thanks."

I face Laurita. "That was incredible!" I tell her. "I've been trying to get Eva to stop for like a year."

Laurita slumps and throws the ball up in the air, catching it in her own mitt. "No surprise."

"What's gotten into you?" I complain. "You've been in a bad mood ever since you got here."

She stares at me. "You don't know?"

"No." *I'm* the one who should be in a bad mood. I'm the one who accidentally told her best friend a huge secret, then discovered that said best friend has not-so-nice opinions and maybe doesn't think I even deserve to live in this whole country.

Laurita shakes her head disgustedly. "You're a wimp, Sofía."

"A wimp?"

"Yeah. You've been talking nonstop about your friend Mrs. Lewis moving into that building, but could you open your mouth for even one second at that meeting to defend her?"

I open my mouth, then shut it again. "Well—I—" I sputter.

"Of course you couldn't," Laurita goes on. "Because you would never disagree with Tricia's mom. You treat every one of Mrs. Rivera's rules like it's unbreakably perfect."

No, I think, it's that Mrs. Rivera treats *Tricia* like she's unbreakably perfect. And as I think that, I realize that I used to treat Tricia that way too. I would give her the costume she likes best without her even having to ask for it. When she said things that hurt me, like that I talked too much about Cuba, I would just keep my head down and say nothing. My insides churn and wriggle as Laurita's words sink in.

But Laurita isn't done yet. "You do an activity you don't even *like* because you're too chicken to tell your family. You could spend some time actually working on our exhibit—"

"I have been working on it!" I blurt out.

"Did *you* do any research on Acorn Corners?"

Oh. All that information Laurita had at the meeting—detailed stuff about taxes and things like that—she got by herself. I've just been putting puff paint on the posters she already made. Also by herself. I hang my head.

Laurita still isn't done. "You could do a million useful things. You could do an activity you actually like. But *no*, Sofía Acosta has to be a ballerina."

"*What* other activities could I do? Mr. Fallon's party is going to be over before break, and it's not like I'm a softball star like you are."

"You could find something," Laurita says. "Take a sewing class. But honestly? I couldn't care less. If you want to be miserable as a ballet dancer, go for it. But if you can't even open your mouth to help someone, then, well—" Laurita scoops her ball up and walks off, shaking her head as she goes down the driveway.

I stand there, a mix of stunned, angry, and sad. Stunned at all of Laurita's words. Angry that she told me off. Sad that I know she's right. I should have said something at that meeting today. I should have worked on the Acorn Corners research ages ago.

CHAPTER THIRTY-THREE

The day before Álvaro's big performance at the Met, Mr. Fallon points to the journal prompt on the board. It says: *Write about what makes your family special.*

I pick up my notebook and flip to a blank page. Of course, it's obvious what makes my family special, and I automatically start writing, *We are a family of ballet dancers.*

I'm about to scribble down the whole story of how my mom and dad were in the Ballet Nacional de Cuba and all the different parts Regina and Manuel and I have had in Mrs. Jansen's shows, but then I notice Tricia chewing on her pencil.

Suddenly I really want to talk to her. We haven't spoken since that day on the UPS and FedEx boxes, but I whisper, "What are you writing about?"

"I don't know," Tricia whispers back, as if nothing ever happened. "Maybe about going to the Cape?"

Tricia's family goes to Cape Cod for a week every summer. Once they brought me with them for the last weekend of their trip—my parents drove me up and then I came back to Pine Hills with the Riveras. It was fun to be with Tricia, but I remember the water being cold and the sand being gritty. Also, a weekend is a long time to go without dessert, which Tricia's family doesn't even have on vacation.

"That's a fun thing to write about," I say, following Tricia's lead and pretending everything is normal.

"You think so?" Tricia asks a little nervously, like she's waiting for my opinion before writing.

"It is," I reply warmly. Tricia picks up her pencil, and while a part of me wonders if vacations are really what makes a family special, I don't say it out loud. I just let Tricia be happy that she has something to write about. I guess that's the way it is now. Tricia and I have to tiptoe around each other so that we don't accidentally talk about something we disagree on, like the apartment building, or Álvaro moving to the United States.

I turn back to my own work and look at what I've written. Then I take my pencil, flip it upside down, and start erasing.

Where it once said *We are a family of ballet dancers,* I write, *We are a family that helps other people, including other immigrant families.* I write about how my mom always keeps snacks for our friends even if they only come over once a week, and about how Davy practically lives at our house, and about how we always have people visiting, so someone is always sleeping on the floor. I add, *Our family is like an accordion—there is al-*

ways room for more people to love inside of it, because it expands and stretches. I smile at what I've written. That Davy is pretty smart.

Then, with a final glance at Tricia and a smirk on my face, I add, *We are Cuban, and we're proud of it. We like to talk about it.*

I close my notebook and fold my hands on top of it. If Mr. Fallon calls on me, I'm ready to share with the class.

CHAPTER THIRTY-FOUR

I cross the street, scuffing my feet on the pavement as I go. I just dropped off some posters for our exhibit at Laurita's house. She's getting them all organized and ready for Mr. Fallon's party tomorrow. I didn't add as many decorations as I meant to, but I pulled together an Acorn Corners poster really quickly. I didn't have any time to make it special; it's just marker. And I didn't have any of the fancy information Laurita had found. It just says IMMIGRANTS NEED SPACE, which is what we already have on another poster. Hopefully no one will notice. I also need to turn the "How Kids Can Help Immigrants" list into a pretty poster like I promised. I tell myself I'll work on it this afternoon. I have some free time before we need to get changed for Álvaro's show.

At home, Regina is practicing in the living room, with Yolanda and Mami guiding her. I head down to the basement and settle into my hiding spot behind the boiler. I put Mr. Rumpkins, Jingle, and Solarie on my lap and talk to them for a few minutes. I meant to work on the poster, but instead I pull out the cardboard theater I made months ago, way back when I was in *Nutcracker* rehearsals, and start working on it again. I use some seed beads and the tiniest paintbrush I can find. When my dad calls to everyone that it's time to get ready, I set the theater down and admire it. It's detailed and realistic, and I'm tempted to bring it upstairs to show Regina. But then she might realize that she never saw me actually make the theater, and find out about my hiding spot. So I say goodbye to my stuffed animals and head upstairs.

Everyone in my family stands on the steps to wave to Yolanda as she leaves for the train station. She has only a dance bag over her shoulder, but her suitcase is packed by the door. I imagine her silently helping the dancers with their costumes for the big performance at the Metropolitan Opera House tonight, knowing what's coming. Tomorrow morning after the show, Yolanda will fly back to Cuba with the rest of the dancers from the Ballet Nacional de Cuba, and Álvaro will stay in New York, officially becoming a defector. As I watch Yolanda shrink away, she looks older than she did when she first came to visit.

As soon as Yolanda is out of sight, Regina goes back inside, and for once she doesn't glide around the house—I can hear her running up the stairs, because she doesn't have a moment to waste. She needs a full three hours to do her hair, do her makeup, and get dressed to see the ballet tonight. It's not very often that my parents take us to see American Ballet Theatre—tickets are so expensive—but when they do, Regina takes how she looks walking into the Met *very* seriously. I love it because we can pretend we're going to a fancy grand ball hosted by kings and queens.

Manuel goes around to the backyard to squeeze in some more playtime before he has to get ready, and I follow my parents back into the house. My mom sighs as we make our way to the kitchen. "I hope Yolanda and Álvaro make up tonight," she says to my dad in Spanish. "It's going to be a long time before they see each other again."

"Yolanda will come visit, though, right?" I ask anxiously.

My mom puts her arm around my shoulder. "Eventually. You know how difficult it is to come here from Cuba."

Thinking about visas and parents who can't visit their kids and abuelas who can't come to the United States makes my insides feel squeezed and tight. "I bet Álvaro will miss Yolanda. Once he gets over being mad at her for telling him not to move."

"De acuerdo. But it's hard not to be mad at your kids when they make decisions that disappoint you, and Yolanda really wanted Álvaro to stay with her in Cuba."

I nod.

"Don't be sad, Sofía," my dad says. "Parents usually find

a way to be with their children. You'll see." He takes my arms and starts dancing salsa. I halfheartedly dance along with him as he sings out a beat. While my feet move, never quite in time with his, I think about what I want to tell my parents. I think I've made a decision, but I don't want to disappoint them. I don't want them to be upset like Yolanda was upset with Álvaro.

"¡Sonríe!" my dad calls mid-dance, reminding me that dancers should always smile as they move. For his sake, I pull up the corners of my mouth and swing my head to his music.

The Metropolitan Opera House is in Lincoln Center, which is a big, beautiful plaza in New York City with a bubbling fountain at the center. My mom, Regina, Manuel, and I all pile into a taxi from Grand Central Terminal to Lincoln Center while my dad catches the subway to meet us there. We walk up the broad, shallow steps that lead from the street to the Lincoln Center Plaza, and Regina daintily lifts the skirt of her gauzy dress. I lift my dress a little bit too, even though the skirt only comes down to my knees, so I can pretend I'm Cinderella entering the ball. The Metropolitan Opera House twinkles at the far end of the plaza, its great glass windows illuminated with golden light from crystal chandeliers shaped like many-pointed stars. Two enormous paintings, each three stories tall, hang in the windows. One is mostly red and the other mostly yellow, and on the giant canvases ladies float like mermaids. My dad tells me they were painted by an artist named Marc Chagall, which he tells us every time we come here, and Regina and I argue about which painting is the best. I like the yellow one, and she likes the red. Manuel jumps up to the edge of the fountain and runs around it in a circle, leaping over people who are taking photos around the fountain and making everyone laugh.

It turns out a lot of our neighbors have bought tickets to the performance. Pine Hill is a small town, and it's not every day that someone people have met before is in a performance at the Metropolitan Opera House. Teresa and Alejandro meet us in front of the fountain, and so does Mrs. Sánchez, Laurita's mom. Her husband and Laurita stayed at home. Even Davy's parents hired a babysitter so they could come. Everyone is dressed up, and we take a million photos in front of the Chagall paintings.

Tricia is there with her parents, and she runs up to me. It still surprises me that she doesn't even realize how angry I am. It's like talking about immigration didn't even matter to her. I grab her arm and pull her away from the Pine Hill crowd.

"Hey, can I ask you something?"

"What?" Tricia's brow wrinkles, and I can tell she's worried that I'm about to talk about a touchy subject again. And I am, but not in the way she thinks.

"Did you tell your mom about Álvaro defecting?" I whisper.

"Of course not!"

"You didn't?"

"I wouldn't do that," Tricia says stiffly. "You said it was a secret."

"I know, but—at the town hall—"

Tricia flips her hair over her shoulder. "Just because we don't agree on that stupid apartment building doesn't mean I'm a tattletale, Sofía."

"No, I didn't think it did mean that. I just thought—"

"You thought I would rat you out."

I'm relieved and confused all at once. I don't know what this means. If Tricia is keeping my secret but she's not on my side, are we still best friends? Then a question pops up in my mind, and I ask:

"Remember how you said Álvaro shouldn't move here because it would mean taking a job from an American citizen?"

"Yeah."

"Why don't you mind that *Mr. Fallon* is an immigrant? I mean, someone else could have his job, too, but it doesn't bother you, because otherwise you wouldn't be working so hard on the Decorations Committee."

Tricia slaps her hand to her forehead. "I meant to ask you, do you have those headpieces for Stella and me? I keep forgetting."

I stare at her. "What?"

"I keep forgetting to ask you. Remember you were going to make us some headpieces?"

I do remember, actually. But then I got sick of Tricia and

Stella doing stuff without me, and I decided I would rather spend my craft time working on the exhibit with Laurita and making my cardboard theater. That doesn't sound very nice, though, so instead I say, "I forgot." I'm about to drop it, but then something inside me gets bubbly and angry, and wondering if this is how Laurita feels all the time, I repeat, "You didn't answer my question. Why is it different for Mr. Fallon?"

"It just is," Tricia snaps. "I don't want to talk about it anymore, okay?"

I hold up my hands. "Fine, okay! We won't talk about it."

But all the holding-it-in-and-not-talking-about-it is like a hot-air jet at my feet, and I walk back to my family angrily. I don't know why I bothered to ask Tricia, because I know the answer. It's different for Mr. Fallon because he speaks English, because he didn't cross the border, because he went to college, because his skin is light and his hair is red. It's a little bit because everyone in school loves him, but mostly because Mr. Fallon is white and Álvaro is Latino. That's the reason, and knowing it makes me so angry I could cry. It doesn't even make a difference that Tricia's part Latina too, because Tricia just thinks whatever the other people from that annoying country club think.

I am sick of fitting myself into little boxes and hiding places, broken up into one person who doesn't talk about being Cuban for Tricia and another person for my family and people like Laurita, a person who talks about having immigrant parents and making space for less-rich people to live in Pine Hill.

The performance is about to begin, and my dad ushers us all toward the Met. I hold his hand, and I promise myself: I am not going to be two people anymore, even if it means that Tricia gets angry at me sometimes. Laurita is right. It's time for me to say what I think, and it's up to Tricia to decide what she wants to do about that.

CHAPTER THIRTY-FIVE

Inside the Metropolitan Opera House, the lights dim, and the crystal chandeliers rise into the ceiling. Regina squeezes my hand. She could practically jump out of her seat. She made me give her my program, because she needs to keep hers pristine—when the show is over, we're going to meet the dancers at the stage door and get their autographs. I don't know why Regina needs them *now*, since she's probably going to see the dancers every day this summer. But she was so excited I couldn't say no.

The first part of the performance is *Theme and Variations*, the ballet that George Balanchine choreographed for Alicia Alonso. Since there's no story, I focus on the costumes, counting the layers of tulle on the ballerinas' tutus, and I notice that the colors sort of match the music—bright and beautiful. Next to me, Regina moves her head side to side, and I know she's mimicking the dancers' movements in her mind.

When the curtain comes down for intermission, my dad

asks me if I was able to tell which dancers were from American Ballet Theatre and which were from the Ballet Nacional de Cuba. I hadn't even thought about that—I knew the dancers from the two companies would be performing together, but it didn't occur to me to try to guess who was who. My dad starts droning on about different styles and techniques in Cuba to anyone who will listen, but Regina interrupts him.

"Papi," she says, "I don't think you have it right."

My dad stops midsentence, looking amused. But he pauses and lets Regina finish what she was saying.

"There's not a Cuban style of dance and an American style of dance," Regina says. "Lots of the dancers from American Ballet Theatre *are* Cuban. ABT has dancers from countries all over the world—but that doesn't make their dancing not American. What makes it American is that the dancers represent so many different cultures around the world. *That's* American."

My dad chuckles. "Well, I stand corrected, then."

Regina crosses her legs and folds her arms daintily. Then she opens up her (my) program to one of the articles in the center. I don't know why they even have those articles. You can't read in a dark theater! Regina hands me back my program.

"You're done with it?"

"No, I need it back, but I wanted to show you this article."

I take my program. I scan the page she was holding open.

It's about an artist whose job it is to make wigs and masks for the dancers at ABT. Not for performances like *Theme and Variations,* but for the big story ballets like *Swan Lake, Coppélia, Sleeping Beauty,* and *The Nutcracker.* The article has pictures of the artist making papier-mâché for a mask and adding twinkling rhinestones to an elaborate wig. Then there's an interview with someone called a costume designer, who gets to decide how all of the different dancers in each performance will look, pick out the materials for the different costumes, and make sketches of each character.

"You could totally do that," Regina tells me.

I flip through the pictures, which show some of the sketches the costume designer makes. It does look pretty cool, and I spend the rest of intermission reading.

"I need that back!" Regina hisses as chimes tinkle throughout the theater, letting people know that intermission is over. Reluctantly, I hand her the program.

When the curtain rises again, it's lots of short numbers, called variations, from different ballets. Álvaro will be dancing a variation from *Swan Lake.* When the music starts for his variation, Regina grips my hand on her left and Manuel's on her right. I reach out and grip my dad's hand, and all of us, the five Acostas, hold hands tightly as Álvaro begins. At first I hold my breath, but once his dancing begins, I relax completely. Álvaro leaps, soars, and spins, his whole body expressing joy and sadness as the music changes from mood to mood, and I have those feelings right along with him. When he takes his bow, we stand up and cheer. Only Álvaro can tell us where he really belongs—whether it's in the United States or in Cuba—but for all of us in the audience, I'm glad he decided it's here.

On the train ride home, our neighbors are so excited about the show that my parents decide to invite them all over for an impromptu party. Mrs. Sánchez calls Laurita and Mr. Sánchez to meet her at our house, and Davy's parents tell the babysitter they'll be home late. I hear my mom whispering to my dad that a late-night party might distract Yolanda, who stares out the window as the train chugs toward Pine Hill. I ask my mom to text the Riveras, since they drove and don't know we're having a party, but Mrs. Rivera says it's too late.

At home we turn on all the lights, and I help my mom find whatever we have in the refrigerator and bring it out to the living room. We have to pull out some of the furniture from the corners, but no one seems to mind. Regina gets permission from Davy's mom to go to his house and pick him up—she carries him into our living room still half asleep in his footed pajamas, and holds him cuddled up to her while she sways in time to the music that my dad blasts from his phone. Even Yolanda starts to cheer up, lost in conversation with Teresa.

Laurita strides across the living room toward me. I stand upright, a little nervous as she gets closer.

"How was the show?" she says.

"Good," I answer cautiously. "I read this article in the program. It was about a costume designer."

Laurita looks at me like she's taking my measurements, figuring me out. "You would be good at that."

"Yeah," I say. "I guess I would be." Then, thinking now is my moment, I say, "I'm sorry I didn't stand up for you at the town hall meeting. I meant to—it's just I got scared because you know Tricia—"

Laurita rolls her eyes. "—is your best friend. Yeah, I've heard it before, Sofía."

I was about to tell Laurita that Tricia *used* to be my best friend, that she has always *been* my best friend but now I'm not so sure she is anymore. That used to scare me. But somehow today it doesn't seem as frightening. But Laurita doesn't let me finish. Instead, she changes topics abruptly.

"So do you have that last poster ready? For Mr. Fallon's party tomorrow."

"Tomorrow?"

Laurita raises an eyebrow. "Yeah, *tomorrow.*"

"Uh—wow, tomorrow is soon."

Now Laurita's eyebrows are scrunched together like she's trying to turn me into stone with her stare. "Did you *forget*?"

"No! I just—"

"Unbelievable."

"I've had a lot going on!"

"Oh yes, the pretty ballerina is much too busy to make a poster about helping other people."

"Hey!"

"What?"

"You can't call me a pretty ballerina that way. You make it sound like ballerinas are weak or something."

Laurita stomps her foot. No one can hear her over the music, but she's almost shouting now. "I wouldn't think that if you didn't act that way. We've been working on this project for months and this was the one thing you were supposed to do. It's the most important poster in the entire exhibit. Otherwise it's just a bunch of facts—we need this poster to show people that they can take action. You knew that, Sofía."

"I know, I just—"

Laurita doesn't even let me finish. "Forget about it. I'll make the poster. I don't need you sticking a bunch of beads to it anyway."

"I thought you liked my decorations!"

"Not if you never actually say any *words*, Sofía!" Laurita shakes her head disgustedly, then marches across the room to Mr. and Mrs. Sánchez. I watch her pretend to be sleepy and Mrs. Sánchez say goodbye to my mom so they can head home. Then I leave the living room and go upstairs while the party downstairs continues. They're all dancing salsa now.

I'm lying in bed feeling horrible about the poster I forgot to make when I hear Regina shriek like she's seen a snake. I jump up and run into the hallway. Regina is still screaming, so I follow her voice toward the bathroom at the end of the hallway.

"I can't make it stop! It's everywhere!" she yells. I push open the door to the bathroom, and I find her crying and shouting, standing ankle-deep in water that's spouting from the toilet.

"What happened?"

"I just flushed—and all of a sudden my dress is ruined!" she wails.

"I'm going to get Mami and Papi." I race down the stairs. I have to shout over the music, but finally my dad hears me.

"Sorry, everyone," he says, stopping the music on his phone. "Just a sec."

While my mom offers all of our guests more snacks, my dad runs up the stairs after me. He dives toward the toilet and spins a knob near the floor, but the water doesn't stop. "I'm calling the plumber," he says, running his hand through his hair nervously. "And let me check the basement."

I help Regina change into clean, toilet-water-free pajamas, and then we go down to the basement to see what my dad is up to. I guess our guests got kind of interested, because the basement is full of people. Even though the Sánchezes and Davy's parents went home, Teresa, Alejandro, Yolanda, Manuel, Regina, my mom, and my dad make quite a crowd.

"The plumber said to look for the main pipe while we wait for him," my dad says. "Not that I have any idea what that is or where it would be."

"Look near the boiler," Teresa suggests, and everyone moves in a group toward it. I start to get nervous.

"Wait!" I say. "Shouldn't we wait for the plumber before—you know—poking around?"

"If he takes much longer, we're going to have water coming through the ceiling," my dad says, and in seconds his flashlight is shining around the boiler, and I hear him say, "What the—" His head disappears around the side of the boiler. He's found my hiding spot, and my mom isn't far behind him.

"What is this?" my mom asks, slipping past my dad. She's thinner than he is, and she easily fits in my space. I dart forward and follow her in.

"What is it?" Teresa calls.

"Nothing related to the water," my mom calls back. We stand there, she and I, and my mom turns in place, taking in everything in my hidey-hole: the stuffed animals I was supposed to donate to the church years ago, the Barbie dolls dressed up as Party Scene girls, the cardboard theater I built. My mom bends down and picks up one of the Barbies. She fingers the lace on the doll's costume.

"Sofía, ¿y esto qué es?"

I burst out crying.

"Pero, Sofía, ¡no es para tanto! Why are you crying?"

"Because—because I know you're going to be mad at me because I didn't donate this stuff to the church!"

My mom looks baffled. "I—well, mi cielo, I would have rather you didn't lie to me, pero—"

"I need a place to practice my sewing! And to keep stuff longer if I still want to play with it. I just—" I sigh, then take a deep breath. I hear Laurita telling me that she liked my decorations, but not if I didn't use actual words. I need to find words, and I need them now. "Upstairs," I explain, "when I'm in the rest of the house, I have to be Sofía Acosta, ballerina."

My mom sets the Barbie down and studies me closely.

"Everyone in our family is a dancer. Regina is headed to ABT, and we know Manuel isn't far behind. But it doesn't matter how hard I try—and I promise it's not because I'm spoiled or not practicing and working hard—I'm just not a ballerina. I'll never get into ABT, or any other dance company for that matter, and everyone knows it. It's embarrassing."

"Sofía, what does that have to do with all this mess?"

"It's not a mess! That's what I'm trying to tell you."

"Pues, espabílate and tell me what all this stuff is, Sofía."

"It's—it's like this. You know how Cubans are all supposed to be great dancers?"

My mom raises an eyebrow. "Cuba is famous for its rhythms," she agrees.

"Well, since I've been friends with Laurita, I've learned some things. Like, did you know Cuba isn't only famous for its music and dance? A lot of famous baseball players come from Cuba, too—not just ballet dancers."

Suddenly my mom bursts out laughing.

"What?"

"You thought I didn't know about Cuban baseball players, Sofía?"

"Well, you're mostly interested in ballet—"

My mom laughs hysterically again. "I'm Cuban, Sofía. I

can know about ballet and baseball. Both of those things are important to us!"

"Yeah. Well. That's it, then. I'm not a baseball star *or* a ballet star, but I'm still Cuban. I'm still an Acosta. Laurita said—" I try to remember her words exactly, but I'll just have to find my own. "People make it seem like you have to be special to belong. Like you have to have a super talent to be Latina and live in Pine Hill. Or like you need to be famous to immigrate to the United States. So if you're like me, and you're not really talented—"

"Sofía," my mom interrupts. "You're very talented. Maybe not at hop-stepping, but at other things—"

"But I don't care," I blurt out. "It's not about being good at stuff. I just want to be an Acosta, and be Cuban, and live in Pine Hill, and not have to earn it by doing ballet."

My mom's face, usually so full of laughter and kisses, is serious. "So—no Mrs. Jansen?"

I shake my head, then hold my breath.

"Okay," my mom says slowly. "Okay, mi cielo. I'm surprised—you've been dancing ballet since you were a little girl and you've never complained—but you don't have to do anything you don't want to do."

"I thought I had to do ballet to be a part of this family. But now I think maybe our family is about more than just ballet."

My mom throws her arms around me. "Sofía, you'll be a part of this family no matter what you do. Ay, mi amor," she says. "I love ballet. But what makes us family is our amor y cariño—*not* ballet."

I know that now. Mr. Fallon helped me learn that by having me write journal entries about what's important to me and what makes my family unique. Seeing my parents try to help Yolanda and Álvaro, and stand up to some of their good friends and neighbors at the town hall meeting, taught me that the Acosta family is about a lot more than just dance. Relief washes over me. Telling my mom how I really feel about ballet wasn't as scary as I thought it would be. My mom looks me up and down, half laughing, half sad.

"Now can you explain all these dolls to me?" she asks. "You stopped playing with dolls years ago."

"Mami," I say. "Do you think Mrs. Jansen needs a junior costume designer?"

My mom takes my face in both her hands and kisses my cheeks. I'm sure there are red lipstick stains all over me now.

"After those Party Scene dresses, how could she not?"

"You liked them? But you always told me to stop goofing off on costumes and focus on the hop-step!"

My mom says, a little sheepishly, "We were pretty distracted these last few weeks—"

"—grooming Regina for future stardom," I finish, and my mom laughs.

"But Party Scene never looked better, Sofía. Really. I meant to tell you."

That's when the doorbell rings, and my mom and I both cock our heads to the side, listening above. Someone opens the front door, and Álvaro's voice pierces the air.

"Mamá," he says, loud enough to be heard through the ceiling rafters, "tenía que despedirme. I don't care if you're mad at me, but I have to follow my passion—our passion. I want to dance with American Ballet Theatre. Pero todavía te quiero, con el alma."

I hear Yolanda reply loud and clear, in her accent that mirrors my own mother's, "Ay, Álvaro, it's—I shouldn't have been mad. I'll miss you so much. But you don't have to live in Cuba to make me happy."

My mom pulls me into a hug, wrapping her arms around my head. She buries her face in my hair. "And you don't have to be a dancer to make me happy, Sofía Acosta."

CHAPTER THIRTY-SIX

"You mean you're not going to take ballet lessons at all?"

The plumber came and fixed our pipes, and told my parents to stop having so many people over at our house, because it's not good for the plumbing. I think my parents are probably going to ignore that advice. It wouldn't be the Acosta Accordion without tons of people. It's after midnight, but Regina and I are still sitting up at the kitchen table, having chocolate milk and Chips Ahoy cookies while my parents and Álvaro help Yolanda with some last-minute packing. Teresa and Alejandro went home, and Manuel is fast asleep upstairs.

"Nope. No ballet. I'm going to ask if I can be Mrs. Lewis's official costume design helper. Then I can just worry about costumes and decorations but not upbeats and downbeats. I won't step on anyone's feet."

Regina shakes her head. "I can't believe it. I told Mami there was no way you were serious about giving up ballet. That's the only time you'll get to see Tricia."

"I'll still see her some of the time," I say. "If I'm working on costumes. But—" I bite my lip. "I think Tricia and I might not be best-best friends anymore."

I dunk my cookie in my milk moodily. I should feel happy and relieved. Everything has worked out. Álvaro and Yolanda aren't fighting, tomorrow my mom is going to text Mrs. Jansen to tell her I'm not coming to ballet classes anymore, and my parents didn't even tell me to get rid of my hiding spot in the basement. Actually, they didn't really say anything about it. But instead of feeling happy, I'm kind of down.

"What's going on?" Regina asks.

I sigh. "I guess it still makes me sad about Tricia. She was my best friend for my whole life, and now it's like we're still friends but I can't talk about some things around her."

"Like what?"

"Like the new apartment building, or some things about being Cuban. Tricia doesn't know what it's like waiting for someone you love to get a visa. And she's always talking about the country club, and she never thinks it's awkward that Mami and Papi can't afford it."

Regina shrugs. "I'd never expect Tricia to be good at talking about that stuff. She's always been a little spoiled, Sofía. You need another friend for those things."

I mash my cookie in the milk with my spoon, making a sort of cookie-milk smoothie. "I had one," I say, "but now we're in a fight because I wouldn't speak my mind—because

I was worried about upsetting Tricia. Basically I just messed everything up."

"Who is the other friend?" Regina asks curiously.

And over cookies and milk, I explain the whole story about the exhibit Laurita and I were planning, and how I didn't back her up at the town hall meeting, even though I meant to, because I was too afraid of Mrs. Rivera, and how I forgot to make the "How Kids Can Help Immigrants" poster for our exhibit because I was so distracted by the Met and everything else, and how now Laurita doesn't really like me anymore, even though she's the one person who ever really *got* me.

Regina shakes her head. "Sofía Acosta. You can solve this problem. If you can practice ballet at five in the morning just to make Mami and Papi happy, sew a zillion tiny beads onto my dance costumes just so I look pretty, and keep the biggest secret of the century—"

"I didn't actually keep that secret—I told Tricia," I remind Regina.

"Well, then now is your chance to make things right. Take all that effort you put into making Tricia happy. But this time do what's better for your family and your real friends. Do what's better for *you*."

CHAPTER THIRTY-SEVEN

In all fairness to Tricia and Stella, the gym looks awesome. There are red-white-and-blue balloons and a professional banner that says CONGRATULATIONS, MR. FALLON! I have a feeling their moms might have helped with buying the balloons and getting the banner printed, but it still looks great. Stella and Tricia have red-white-and-blue hair ribbons that match Lucas's and Abdul's wristbands. They don't look as good as the headpieces I would have made, but they're okay. Anyway, I didn't want to make them myself.

I drag my parents around the gym, showing them each part of the exhibit Laurita and I made.

"So do you still think we came here from Ellis Island?" my dad asks, elbowing me with a laugh.

I shake my head and read him the Ellis Island poster. We make our way around the exhibit, my parents' faces growing more serious as they read the poster about border crossings and ICE. But when they get to the very end of the exhibit, they both break out laughing, and they pat me on the back.

Bedazzled with every bead and rhinestone in my collection, so that the words stand out bright and bold, is the poster about how kids can help immigrants, which I stayed up late making just the way Laurita and I planned. And next to that poster, with even bolder and louder and clearer words, is another poster. It reads:

ONE THING YOU CAN DO: SUPPORT ACORN CORNERS!

I listed all the reasons the new building would help our community and underlined this passage: *This building will make Pine Hill a more diverse and welcoming community. Some of the people who move to the building will have unique talents, and some of the people will be great friends and neighbors. They will make Pine Hill a better place to live.*

My parents have me pose for a photo next to the poster. Across the gym, Tricia is watching us. She's with her mom, who is slicing a cupcake in half and placing one of the halves carefully on a plate for Tricia. For a second, I get nervous, but then I shake it off and look right at the camera and smile for my parents. Tricia is allowed to disagree with me. But no one is allowed to stop me from saying what I believe.

I've just finished taking photos with my Acorn Corners poster when Stella comes running up and taps me on the shoulder.

"Your posters are really good." She says it all at once, like she's in a rush to get the words out. "I think you're right about Acorn Corners and I meant to say so but I didn't know what to say at the Modern Manners party because I didn't want to be mean to Tricia and—"

Stella stops abruptly, like she ran out of air, or things to say. Or excuses.

I almost brush her off. I almost say it doesn't count to tell me now if she couldn't say it in front of anyone else. Then Stella adds:

"I wish I were brave like you. I wish I could say stuff."

Then I get it. "I'm not really brave," I explain. "I just got lucky—Mrs. Kalinack assigned me to Laurita's committee." Stella might have the country club, she might be Tricia's new best friend, she might be the next Regina-level ballerina in Pine Hill. But this time, I'm the lucky one.

"Attention! Up here!" Mrs. Kalinack claps out a rhythm from the mic at the front of the gym, and we all clap back. She pulls out her phone. "I just got a text message that Mr. Fallon is in the parking lot. Are we ready?"

"READY!"

The door opens, and in walks my favorite teacher of all time. Mrs. Kalinack hands him an American flag, which clashes terrifically with his bright orange hair, and the expression on his face is total and complete surprise. We cheer and hoot and Mr. Fallon laughs with joy.

It seems like there are a million people Mr. Fallon has to shake hands with. It takes him a while to get to the end of the exhibit, where my parents and I are still waiting.

"Wow! Did you do this all by yourself, Sofía?"

"No," I say honestly. "Laurita did most of the work, and my sister, Regina, helped me too." Then I add, "But I believe everything here. Even if people don't think I'm right about Acorn Corners, I still wanted to put it on a poster. Because *I* think it's the right thing to do."

Mr. Fallon holds out his hand for a fist bump and motions for his boyfriend to come look at my poster.

I head toward the snack table and find Laurita standing with her hands in her pockets and a wistful smile on her face. "Hi," she says.

"Hi," I say.

"The exhibit is pretty great," Laurita says. "Lots of people are telling me they read every poster."

"I know!" I take a deep breath. "I'm sorry I didn't do more work sooner. I shouldn't have waited until the last minute."

"It's okay. You're the one who made everything look amazing. You're so good at this stuff, Sofía. No one would have paid attention to my boring posters."

"Not a chance," I agree, grinning.

Laurita holds up her mitt. "Want to go outside and throw some balls?" She leads the way out of the gym. "You're pretty good for someone who's never been on a team. It must be the Cuban in you!"

I shake my head. "Don't believe everything you hear about Cubans. Some of us have two left feet, you know."

Laurita roars with laughter and tosses me the ball, even though we're inside and Mrs. Kalinack might kill us. As we head outside to play some proper catch, I think how good it is to have a friend like Laurita, one who throws me the hard balls and makes me speak my mind.